THE DATING DILEMMA

A LOVE BUG NOVEL
BOOK 2

KELLY COLLINS

BOOK NOOK PRESS

CHAPTER ONE

LIV

I stand facing the door of the famed eatery, La Lumière, thinking about the convoluted web of connections that brought me here. Sure, I hailed a cab, but this seems like it's straight out of a sitcom's blooper reel. Never in my wildest dreams did I think I'd end up in this restaurant on a blind date, thanks to my hairdresser's brother's yoga instructor's dog walker, but here I am.

Most would consider me lucky, with two parents who adore me, a bank account that never stops growing, and a closet bursting with beautiful designer clothes that would be the holy grail of any so-called influencer. Yet, in still moments, when the laughter of my friends has quieted and faded and the city's lights dim, I feel the gaping void in my life—a void that no amount of wealth or fabulous attire can fill. It's as though I've collected all the stars in the night sky but missed the one that would light up my heart. For all intents and purposes, I'm a cat lady in waiting. I pause at the door and pray Mr. Right is inside. I'm not sure I could handle being stood up on a blind date.

A deep breath and a death grip on the door handle, and I'm inside. A shimmer of hope lightens my heart. The place is beautiful. Chandeliers bathe the polished tables in a dreamy pastel light while music from a live pianist sets an unexpectedly carefree and upbeat mood. This could be it. It has to be better than that impromptu smooch with the pizza delivery guy, which, embarrassingly enough, led to a bout of mono.

As I'm guided to our table, my breath catches in my throat at the sight before me. My date's commanding presence and striking features take my breath away. At least I hope he's my date because the only other man sitting alone is about forty years my senior and seems uninterested in anything but what's on his plate. I'm not sure he can even see it through the two-inch Coke bottle lenses on his glasses, a real blind date. The man I'm laser-focused on is tall and regal with a strong jawline and piercing blue eyes that seem to see right through me. And thank God, he's actually looking at me. Every detail of his appearance radiates confidence and charm, from the perfectly styled dark hair to the impeccably tailored suit that fits him like a Givenchy model on a Milan runway. Holy hell, this guy is something to look at. What if looks are all he has? Or he has bad manners? Now, I'm getting ahead of myself. *Try not to tank the only date you've had in months before you even sit down, Liv.*

"Hello," he says and my knees wobble—who am I kidding, they practically buckle at his greeting. Is "hello" usually so sumptuous? His presence is dazzling, a tidal wave of attraction that steals my breath the way it happens in movies. He's the type of man that makes you forget your name, a dashing stranger so impressive that even a guard dog would surrender their tough exterior for a belly rub in his presence. His air of sophistication and refinement could win over anyone, even convincing the stubborn moon to dim its light for a romantic porch-side dinner with him.

As he says, "Olivia," my name rolls off his tongue like a familiar melody. Our fingers brush as we shake hands, sending a zing straight through me.

"Seb," I say, "it's funny how the universe works, isn't it? One connection leads to another, and here we are."

A rich and warm chuckle parts his lips and reveals two broad rows of perfect teeth even more beguiling than his broad shoulders and chiseled jawline. "It's that six degrees of separation thing, isn't it? Although I never expected it would bring me here tonight either."

I can already detect the change in the air between us. This date will be different, I feel it. If not, I vow to become a nun. But then I imagine a closet full of a nun's habits instead of Dolce and Gabbana or Gucci and quickly dismiss that thought. My mother would never stand for it if I wasn't dressed in premier designers from head to toe. Gucci doesn't design clothes for the cloistered. And, I don't know how many cats you can have in a nunnery.

Seb leads me to my seat with effortless grace, taking

his own across from me. "I've ordered the chef's tasting menu and wine pairings. I'm sure you'll enjoy it."

"Oh, that sounds, um, delightful." I try my best to mask my surprised disappointment, but I'm clearly struggling to keep up the facade. It's always been a point of contention when someone assumes they know what I will or won't like and robs me of my choices. My dietary restrictions and picky eating habits have caused more than a few awkward moments, but I try to remain open-minded. In the worst case, I'll drink the wine, a lovely cabernet already poured into goblets.

His face lights up. "You have to try the foie gras. It's a specialty here."

My heart sinks at the thought, and without meaning to, I blurt, "I volunteer and donate monthly to the Lucky Duck Sanctuary."

He raises an eyebrow. "Oh?"

"I support rescued ducks," I clarify, needing to explain myself. "Eating one, let alone, just its fattened liver, would feel like eating my young."

I watch the play of emotions across Seb's face—surprise, then a flicker of amusement. He recovers quickly, suggesting another dish. "Well, perhaps the caviar?"

I hesitate for a moment too long before admitting, "Actually, I'm vegan."

"Of course, you are!" There's a brief pause as Seb processes this information. "What was I thinking?" My cheeks heat in embarrassment. "I should have asked first."

Internally, I'm nodding in agreement, but outwardly,

I shrug my shoulders nonchalantly. "Really, I should have told you. I'm just used to scouring menus and putting together the puzzle of what I can eat. Vegan is a choice."

"If you would have said something, I could have made other arrangements," he says with a kind look on his face.

He waves the server over and whispers something to him. The server nods eagerly before scurrying off, leaving me curious about what just happened.

Seb's smile widens, dimples etching his cheeks. "Forget the tasting menu. Tonight's a vegan adventure, and the server leads the way."

"That's very kind." My heart hums in gratitude, feeling that his gesture is a good omen. Rarely does someone navigate so graciously the garden path of self-imposed dietary restrictions with me. His ready acceptance and the quick pivot alone plants a seed of fondness for him.

"Always a vegan or something you're trying out?"

"I've been one since I won a barbecue cook-off at a county fair while visiting my cousin Beatrice in Iowa. They crowned me the "Pig-Out Princess" after eating enough ribs, bacon, and pulled pork to feed an army. The meat sweats did it to me, but if they hadn't, the looks I got from the 4-H hogs would have. They gave me that side-eye of judgment. It was as if they knew I'd just wolfed down their second cousin twice removed. Every time I glanced at a pork chop, I sensed those piggy eyes watching me—it was the universe's signal that change was needed. One thing leads to another."

"I'm impressed. Veganism takes real commitment."

"Thank you," I say, my gratitude mingling with a resolve to recover from the rocky start to the meal. I catch myself almost launching into the kind of interrogation that would make my mother proud—"So, what do you do? Where did you study?" The mental image of her interviewing my date as if he's a candidate for marriage makes me inwardly cringe. No, I won't subject Seb to that. Besides, I want our conversation to sparkle with curiosity, not the dull patina of routine. Instead, I try to steer the conversation toward more interesting things.

"So, what's your soundtrack?" I venture, hoping music might be a safer topic. He perks up, the way people do when they're about to unleash their "cool" playlist.

"Indie bands are my jam. Ever hear of The Silent Whispers?"

I draw a blank, which is probably a sin in the indie world. "Nope, but if they ever do a duet with Taylor Swift or Ed Sheeran, they'll be on my radar." I offer a playful wink.

He laughs, a rich baritone that fills the space between us. "I guess you're the one turning up the radio for the Top 40 hits, huh? As for me, if it's played in more than three coffee shops, it's too mainstream for my taste."

I giggle, imagining him with a secret life as a coffee shop DJ, scornfully skipping any track that's ever seen the light of a Billboard chart.

"Hmm," I muse, giving him my best "thoughtful" look, which is really just me trying not to squint. "Movies—please don't break my heart. Tell me you're a secret rom-com fanatic?"

He takes a contemplative sip of wine, his smirk suggesting he's about to shatter my Hugh Grant dreams. "Thrillers, actually. Ever seen *The Shining*?" He grabs his knife, thrusting it in the air like he's warding off a demonic bartender. "'Here's Johnny!'"

I recoil, feigning terror. In fact, I am a little terrified. So far, we have absolutely nothing but cabernet in common. "Watched it once and wore more popcorn than I ate. It's not great armor against ghostly twins. Still suffering cinematic stress disorder."

He leans in, the thrill of fear lighting up his eyes. "I find something ... exhilarating about scaring the wits out of myself."

I flutter my lashes dramatically. "Thrills? Try snatching the last designer bag at a cutthroat sample sale. That's combat with style—and at 70% off, no less." We toast to our different brands of adrenaline.

He chuckles, acknowledging the point. "I'll give you that. But it's hard to beat the suspense of a good thriller for me."

"While you're on the edge of your seat, I'm the girl buried under blankets, crying over a rom-com's grand gesture." I guess gruesome acts befalling someone in a thriller are as unlikely in real life as someone slipping past airport security and proposing in a full airplane. So, we're both unrealistic. That's something we have in common.

He lifts a brow, a challenge in his gaze. "I'm guessing you're not the type to brave the wild?"

I tap my chin in contemplation. "Do you mean having

to ask for feather alternative pillows at a five-star hotel? Braving the wilds of the lobby when the Wi-Fi is down?"

His laughter is loud enough to startle the sommelier. "I'm talking about real camping. You know, where you fish for your dinner and sleep under the stars?"

I shudder dramatically. "Of course, I don't eat fish, so I'd starve, but the only stars I'll sleep under are five at a time on American Express Fine Hotels and Resorts." We lock eyes, a smile playing on his lips.

"You're telling me you've never felt the call of the wild?"

"Just how wild are we talking?" I ask as I ponder our mismatched versions of adventure. I think his idea of a day in the woods could be my version of a horror film.

His smile fades as the server returns with our plates and sets them before us. "Our chef has prepared a vegan quinoa salad with roasted vegetables and a tahini dressing."

Seb's expression turns slightly pale. "Tahini? Of all things, sesame seeds are the one thing I'm allergic to."

My eyes widen in surprise. "You must be joking."

He pushes the plate away, sighing. "I wish I were."

I give him an understanding smile, trying to rescue the situation once more. "Please go ahead and order what you like. You were very nice to arrange a tasting menu, which I know is usually for the entire table. I'll bring the extras home. I never expect everyone to see through my vegan lens. Enjoy your meal, no judgments."

He sighs, and his lips curl into an upward curve. "In

that case..." He glances through the menu briefly before making his selection. "I'll have the ribeye steak, rare."

I nibble on my quinoa salad until his food arrives. His dish is dull compared to my bright and colorful vegan meal. The only color on his plate is red, seeping from the almost raw meat. As he slices into the steak, my stomach churns. It's like a side of Brontosaurus impaled with his steak knife. He *is* a horror junkie. I inhale deeply, refocusing on my food. "Bon appétit." I reach for my water glass, and watch mortified as it topples in slow motion, water cascading out like a flood, oozing across the table, and making a beeline for Seb's lap, drenching his trousers "Oh, no!" I snatch my napkin to dab at the spill, but it grazes the candle's flame. A tiny ember catches, and the napkin ignites. Panicking, I throw the flaming fabric away from us and watch in horror as it lands on another tablecloth and sets it alight. What the heck? Are they washing their linens in kerosene?

As if our evening couldn't get any worse, the smoke ribbons quickly toward the ceiling, activating the fire alarms, and the sprinklers turn on and drench us instantly. My sleek Chanel dress now clings to my body like the wrapper on a melted chocolate bar. And even more horrifically we're not alone. Other diners are caught in this unexpected monsoon, turning their glamorous outfits into ill-fitting swimwear. Michelin star meals and auction-worthy wines are now part of the sudden rainforest drench. The elderly man in the coke bottle glasses is laughing among the gasps and screams of other diners. The intricately carved radish shaped like a rosebud that adorned my "quinoa surprise" is now drifting out to sea with the cabernet and the Brontosaurus.

Despite the surrounding chaos, Seb suppresses a laugh. His suit is now wet and sticking to him like a second skin. It's an attractive visual. "Well, this is definitely one way to make a first impression," he says with a chuckle. "Are you okay?" he asks with genuine concern as we sit amidst the remnants of our disastrous first date dinner.

My cheeks burn with embarrassment as the waitstaff escorts us out of the restaurant, leaving the table fires behind. "Just a typical evening for me," I try to joke, but it falls flat.

We step into the chilly night air and stand there shivering in silence, both a bit stunned by what just happened.

"I would offer you my jacket, but it wouldn't do much good." He looks down at his soaking suit.

"I'll manage," I say, though a tremble betrays me. As if on cue, the sky rumbles, and a thunderous downpour begins, the rain's chill seeping into my already freezing bones.

"Seems luck is not topping our guest list tonight," he says, eyeing the clouds.

"Perhaps the universe is trying to tell us something," I say, wiping raindrops off my face. "Maybe it's time to call it a night."

Seb tilts his head, considering my suggestion. "You might be onto something there. We should probably call it quits while we're ahead."

I laugh. "If this is what you consider ahead, I don't even want to know your definition of failure."

Spotting the neon glow of the Pies Before Guys sign across the street, I decide to treat myself to some comfort food. "I'm going to grab some goodies from that bakery. You can come along if you'd like."

He shakes his head with a sign of resignation. "I don't think I could handle much more excitement tonight. No one is actually hurt yet. I hesitate to imagine what calamities might await in a place where there are hot pies, pastry blades, and ovens in plain sight. I think I'll just head home. Take care, Olivia."

With a wave, I walk away and head toward the bakery, wondering whether the vegan snickerdoodles are really going to make me feel any better. As I enter, the scent of cinnamon and sugar wraps around me like a comforting hug. Eloise is there, as she always is, a steady presence in the ebb and flow of my unpredictable life. She looks up, her knowing eyes meeting mine. "One of those days that make you wish for a do-over, huh, Liv?"

I let out a half-laugh. "More like a do-not-repeat. It was a disastrous date," I reply as I pick out a variety of cookies from the bakery case. "If things were any worse, we'd be on the evening news." And who knows, we still might end up as breaking news. I can already imagine the headline. "Olivia Kato's Love Life: A Sign of the Apocalypse?"

Eloise hands me a cup of tea on the house, her trademark remedy for heartache and headache alike. "Remember, every misstep is just the setup for the moment when everything aligns. You're gathering stories for the great love story that's yet to come."

Her words, light with humor but heavy with truth, make me pause. I take a sip of the tea, letting the warmth spread through me. "Maybe I'm just gathering evidence for my future cats to prove why they're my ultimate soul-mates," I say.

Eloise's laughter fills the bakery. "Darling, even the best bakers have to try a recipe more than once. Keep at it. Your next batch might just be the masterpiece."

"At this rate, that batch will involve wearing a hazmat suit and attending a safety briefing." I pay and tuck the box under my arm—a small salve for a bruised ego, sold with a slice of sage advice.

Outside the bakery, the cool night air brushes my face. I pause, savoring the momentary calm, and then send Junie a message.

Disaster date, but I'm still alive, and he's gone home. We might end up on the city's most-wanted list for causing public distur-bances and endangering others.

Junie responds almost immediately.

Haha! Always an adventure with you. How about a movie night at my place? AJ is working late.

Grinning, I reply.

Count me in. Bring out the rom-coms!

She replies, **Wow, this is serious. I'm opening a good bottle too.**

CHAPTER TWO

SEB

Olivia's retreating silhouette holds me paralyzed, and my thoughts swirl in a combination of disbelief and mild amusement. Am I being a jerk for not going for a cookie? I mean she drenched my pants, set the restaurant on fire, and we were escorted from one of my favorite places after ruining everyone else's dinner too. Admittedly, it was a little exciting. Sure, she's gorgeous with her long black hair and cognac-colored eyes, but trusting a near stranger with my heart?

Doubts continue to swim laps in my head, back and forth, as I watch her disappear into the shop called Pies Before Guys, a name that speaks volumes about its priorities.

Hailing a cab, I slide into the back seat and give the driver my address: 218 38th Avenue. As we drive through the rain, I imagine a world where desserts triumph over dates. Tonight, I would have much rather drowned my sorrows in a wall of chocolate cake instead of ending up with a wet wool suit, an empty stomach, and an emptier heart. Even good dates are like running a gauntlet. This was like being knocked down in one.

Suddenly, the cab hits a pothole and snaps me out of my thoughts. The sound of raindrops tapping against the window echoes the racing musings in my head. Each drop brings back memories, doubts, or glimpses of hope. That neon sign flashes in my mind. *Pies Before Guys*. She said it was a bakery, but the name seems better suited for a club for women or an underground organization for women who don't like men.

As I watch the city's familiar landmarks pass by, my phone vibrates, and Ryan's name appears on the screen. For a moment, I debate whether to answer, but my curiosity gets the better of me, and I swipe to accept the call.

"What's going on?" I ask.

"Hey, Seb. How's the date?" Ryan responds.

"It's done." I sigh. "To say it was a disaster would be an understatement."

Ryan lets out a whistle. "That bad, huh? Did she have four heads, a face like a warthog? Sounds like you need a drink. Want to meet me at The Lighthouse?"

I force a smile, despite being utterly drenched. "Sounds good. I'll head over after I wring myself out."

"Caught in the squall?" he asks.

"You could say that. I'm so wet, there could be fish swimming in my underwear."

"Sounds bad. Usually, you'd want a woman in those," Ryan chuckles. "Go change, and I'll see you soon."

As the taxi winds through the city, the streetlights blur into one another—mirroring the disorganized patchwork of thoughts competing for attention in my mind. Romance is a maze with no exit, it seems.

I sink further into the soft leather seats of the cab, taking in the chaotic beauty of the city as we drive through the rain. "Seems like traffic is heavy tonight," I comment, trying to distract myself from my own thoughts.

The driver nods in agreement. "It always is on a rainy evening. Everyone's rushing to get somewhere."

It's true. We're all in a never-ending race, searching for happiness and success. But sometimes, in our haste, we forget to appreciate the simple things like rain on our skin, the nervous excitement of a blind date, or the thrill of narrowly avoiding disaster. The cab pulls up outside my home in The Avenues. "Do you mind waiting? I'll be quick," I assure the driver as I step out into the darkness of the night.

With a quick flick of the switch, the room is bathed in warm light. The shadows retreat to the corners, creating a sense of comfort and safety. Despite being alone, I'm not lonely. In fact, it's almost a relief not to have to rely on anyone but myself. My experiences with trusting others have left me wary and guarded, especially after losing half my company to a supposed "trusted" partner.

If someone who once called me a friend could do that, how much damage could a romantic partner cause? A shiver runs down my spine.

I trade my drenched suit for dry slacks and a sweater.

The quiet of the house surrounds me, a confirmation of my single status. It seems ... right. Safe.

No, for now, these four walls and this solitude are where I belong. I grab an umbrella and prepare to brave the drizzle outside. Stepping out into the night air, I am greeted with a cool kiss from the wind. Striding toward the waiting cab, its engine humming softly, I take in the sights and sounds of the busy city around me.

A short ride later, we arrive at my destination. The Lighthouse. The driver seems grateful for the large tip, and I step out onto the sidewalk, unfurling my umbrella against the misty rain. As I approach the grand entrance, the door swings open with a welcoming creak. The sounds of lively conversation and clinking glasses invite me inside toward camaraderie and companionship.

I weave through the crowd to the bar and take a seat, my fingers drumming a restless beat on the counter. The bartender, a wiry man with a beard to rival that of the Viking god Thor, gives me a nod. "What can I get you?"

"Whiskey, neat," I reply. "And please keep them coming."

The bartender shoots me a look as if I'd ordered unicorn tears on the rocks. "Rough night?"

"You have no idea," I sigh.

He pours me a drink and I take a swig, trying to drown out the disappointment that lingers in my mind. Ryan appears beside me, slapping me on the back excitedly. "Seb! The man of the hour! Give me all the juicy details." He takes a seat, and I take a gulp. The heat of the alcohol slides down my throat, providing some comfort.

"La Lumiére, Ryan. It was a fancy tasting menu with a romantic atmosphere. Everything was perfect. Until..." I pause and let out a bitter laugh. "She's a vegan. Not just a vegetarian, mind you—a no animal products of any kind sort of eater."

"Ouch. At La Lumiere?" Ryan winces. "That's like bringing a goldfish to a sushi bar."

"She doesn't sleep on feather pillows either. But wait, there's more," I say with growing enthusiasm as I continue my tale of woe. "She loves rom-coms. Who actually watches those willingly? And nature? She has no interest in it. We might as well be from different planets." A snort escapes me. " Did I mention she knocked over a candle and set the table on fire—after accidentally pitching a full glass of water into my lap? And then she walks into Pies Before Guys after leaving me. It was like witnessing her declaration of never wanting another man again, or at least not me."

Ryan raises an eyebrow, clearly amused. "Tables on fire? She sounds hot. Perhaps she's onto something with the bakery. Pies don't argue back or hog the remote."

I laugh. "Well, that's one way to look at it. But really, my dating game needs a serious reboot."

Ryan grins, leaning in conspiratorially. "You need this app." He pulls out his phone and taps until "Love Bug" shows up.

"Seriously? A dating app? Love Bug? Sounds pretty hopeless. I'm already Tinder Cinder and Un-Hinged. Just joking, I've never tried those apps. When have I had time?"

"It's not just any dating app. It's the premiere new dating app."

"What makes it premiere?"

"The app is all about forging meaningful connections, not just superficial ones. Who cares if your date was a vegan? It would only matter if you owned a meat processing plant or were a subsistence survivalist, but neither apply. And as for movies, have you ever heard of compromising? Maybe seeing things from your date's perspective could open your mind."

I nod slowly, mulling over his words. "Okay, okay, I'll think about trying it. But deep connections from a phone app?"

Ryan lets out a laugh. "Surprising, isn't it? But think about it. Sometimes, it's easier to dive into someone's psyche when you're behind a screen. People are more honest and vulnerable. And this app? It facilitates that. It even makes you complete several objectives before allowing you to see the person."

I let out a sigh, twirling the amber liquid in my glass. "But what about the thrill of the chase? The real-life connections, the serendipitous meetings? That initial attraction." My body reacted to Olivia. Every cell was screaming, Systems go! But I just stood there in the rain and watched her walk away.

Ryan leans back, observing me for a moment. "There can be some magic in that when it ends up where you hope. But sometimes, it's like searching for a needle in a haystack. This? It's like a magnet. And hey, even if it doesn't work out, at least you'll have some great stories to share on our next night out."

"So, it's all about the stories now?"

Ryan grins. "Isn't life just a collection of tales? And who knows, Love Bug might give you a chapter worth reading."

His words leave an impression on my mind, and though the concept of finding true love as opposed to a hook-up through an app still confuses me, tonight's lesson is clear. Always expect the unexpected.

I take a deep breath, and three whiskies in, I decide, "Okay. Let's download Love Bug. But if my next date ends up being as chaotic as tonight, I'm sending you the bill."

Ryan raises his glass with a smirk. "Deal! To new adventures, meaningful connections, and ... hopefully, less clumsy dates?"

For the next hour, I fill out the questionnaire while chatting with Ryan about life.

He takes a sip of his drink and leans in closer. "So, how are things going at Innovative Advertising?"

I rub the back of my neck, contemplating the challenges and successes of my job. "Busy as always. We've been searching for an exceptional designer for a while now. Brad took Mia with him when he left."

Ryan's eyebrows shoot up. "And? Did you find anyone promising?"

Pride seeps into my voice as I respond, "Actually, we have. The HR team snagged someone today. Goes by the name Liv Kato. I haven't met her in person yet, but her work is highly recommended. Claire from HR says she designed the graphics for a wildly successful app."

Ryan laughs, taking another sip of his drink. "Sounds like a great addition."

I nod, relieved that the team has found someone who hopefully has the skills we've been missing. That sense of relief quickly turns to a different feeling when my phone dings with my avatar. "What the hell?"

Ryan leans over. "A stag beetle? That's quite the statement."

I shake my head in disbelief. "So, what did this app assign you?"

Ryan reveals his screen to show a radiant firefly. "Behold, the firefly."

We both laugh. I comment, "Ah, the insect known for lighting up even the darkest of nights. How fitting for you."

Ryan grins. "It represents someone who can bring light to any situation, has a knack for creativity and innovation, and is drawn to all things romantic and whimsical."

"Always the hopeless romantic, huh?" I tease.

Ryan just winks in response. "It's ingrained in me. I can't help it."

"And I end up with a beetle for my avatar?"

Ryan laughs heartily. "Hey, at least it's not a stink beetle. Silver lining."

He takes my phone and reads off the attributes of the stag beetle. "'This insect symbolizes leadership and strength.'" Ryan nods approvingly. "'Don't underestimate those prominent jaws—they represent power, strategy, and precision. Plus, the transformation from egg to adult is a metaphor for growth and change.' Sounds like the perfect fit for someone leading Innovative Advertising, right?"

I ponder for a moment before responding. "I have to admit, it's quite fitting. But what speaks to me more is its resilience and adaptability. In the world of advertising, being able to roll with the punches and still see the opportunities is crucial."

Ryan raises his glass in a toast. "To the stag beetle, then. May it guide you to someone equally resilient and forward-thinking."

We clink our glasses together, our shared laughter easing the weight of the night's mishaps. Ryan's infectious optimism reminds me that sometimes, life's biggest surprises are just around the corner.

CHAPTER THREE

LIV

The rain pounds against Junie's building, sounding like an army of drummers searching for a rhythm. As the elevator opens quietly, I stumble out, drenched and sloshing in my high heels. Junie's apartment engulfs me, a chaotic mix of eccentric art and a strangely extensive collection of Vans shoes lined up by the doorway.

"Is that you?" Junie peeks around the corner, her eyes widening at the sight of me. "You look like a drowned cat but smell like a campfire."

I attempt to keep a straight face, but I can only giggle. "Believe me, my night was nothing short of catastrophic."

Her red hair bounces as she approaches me, but the Pies Before Guys box in my grasp causes her eyes to nearly pop out of her head. "You brought cookies?"

"These cookies were a must-have. Especially after my date went from sparks to literal fire," I say, holding up the box. "Think of them as my therapy dessert."

Junie laughs and reaches for the box. "Well, if that's

the case, the worse the date, the better the cookie. Let's open these up and see just how bad your evening was. But first, let me grab you something dry and comfortable to wear."

She guides me past her living room, where she places the cookies on the coffee table, and we walk through her bedroom toward her massive closet. It's hard to believe that just last year, Junie lived in an apartment smaller than her collection of shoes.

Some things never change, especially regarding Junie's closet organization. There are the "daily digs" filled with an array of jeans and trendy T-shirts, the "special maybe" section proudly showcasing her funeral pants, and the "when pigs fly" area stocked with fancy dresses and sky-high heels. Junie's wardrobe is as unique and vibrant as her personality, always at odds with my more conservative taste in fashion. She excitedly pulls out a pair of flannel pants covered in cartoon characters from the daily digs section. "These are perfect!" she exclaims. Then she rummages through her collection of T-shirts, searching for a specific one like she's on a treasure hunt. "Aha! This one is a masterpiece in cotton," she declares, tossing me a shirt that reads, "Hot Mess Express. Chugging Along!" Leave it to Junie to have an outfit for every occasion. Finally, she hands me a pair of fuzzy socks from a drawer, completing her ensemble with coziness and flair.

"You think of everything." I gratefully accept the offered clothing.

But she isn't finished yet. She hands me underpants

and points out the days of the week embossed on them. Wednesday. I narrow my eyes, puzzled.

"These are for Wednesday," I point out.

She winks at me. "I only have one pair of Friday panties, and they are currently in use."

After I change into the clothes she's given me, I flop down onto her plush buttery soft leather couch, relishing the comfort against my exhausted body.

Junie plops down next to me, her excitement clear in her sparkling eyes. "Okay, give me all the details. Start from the beginning and don't leave out any juicy bits."

I eagerly open the box of cookies, grab a chocolate chip one, and take a big bite. I'm starving after my date left me feeling empty, and I need some serious sugar reinforcement to deal with this saga. "Which do you want to hear first, the good or the bad?"

My friend takes a cookie and covers herself in an orange cable knit throw. "A mix of both."

I cross my legs and grab another cookie from the box. Tonight calls for a double-fisted approach. "Before I delve into tonight's disaster, let me start with the only positive. Seb was incredibly attractive to look at."

Junie sits up, interested. "How attractive? Like Khal Drogo from *Game of Thrones* or Brad Pitt from *Fight Club?*"

Our taste in men is not the only thing that sets us apart. "Somewhere between if Bradley Cooper, Ryan Reynolds, and Henry Golding were in a thrupple and had a baby."

Junie's eyes widen, and I retract my previous

thoughts about her taste in men. She can clearly see the potential offspring from that mix. She takes a bite of a cookie, and her eyes shut in pure delight. "Oh, this is heavenly! Sometimes, I think you purposely go on terrible dates just for the after-date treats."

I roll my eyes. "Trust me, no treat is worth enduring what I went through tonight."

She reaches for another cookie and holds up both hands. "I'm prepared for the worst."

"Well," I begin, shifting on the couch. "Imagine this ... you're at one of the fanciest restaurants in town, looking amazing in your new dress. You spot your date, and he's handsome beyond belief. Then, Mr. Right—scratch that —Mr. *Absolutely Wrong*, orders for you like it's 1959 or something."

Junie gasps in mock horror. "No way!"

"Tasting menu," I confirm with a dramatic sigh.

Junie's mouth forms a perfect "O" shape. "How romantic."

"For the right girl, perhaps. But for me ... it's a disaster. The first course is a duck foie gras."

"Did you tell him about the Lucky Duck Sanctuary?"

"Yes, so he asks about caviar." I stick out my tongue and gag. "Then I explain myself, and he kindly orders a vegan menu."

Junie watches me like I'm some kind of reality show, and honestly, she's not too far off.

"That seems very considerate of him."

"It's doused in tahini."

Junie tilts her head. "But you love tahini."

I nod, then wince. "Turns out he's allergic. And to add insult to injury, there was a bloody steak the size of a dinosaur, an overturned water glass, and a literal fire. The rest? A night for the history books. Okay, I will admit that the water, the fire, and the restaurant sprinklers drenching everyone was my fault, but not the torrential rain when we were removed from the restaurant. That's when he left."

Junie grins. "But at least he's easy on the eyes, right?"

I give her a look as though she has grown another head. "That's your main takeaway?"

"Well, let's focus on the positive aspects?"

I raise an eyebrow. "Please enlighten me. What might those be?"

Internally, I am amused and exasperated by Junie's mind. It is a remarkable place that never stops generating the most eccentric ideas.

Without skipping a beat, she lists some with a dramatic flair.

"At least he wasn't an axe murderer—always a good sign. And the spilled water wasn't even wine—so your dress is safe! And hey, with all the chaos, you probably bolted from the scene so quickly that there was no time for that awkward who's paying moment."

"There was a possibility that he could have been an axe murderer, but now I'll never know. We never got to enjoy the wine, and I always pay, so I don't feel oblig-ated to kiss them goodbye. However, tonight, there wasn't time to take care of the bill before we had to evacuate."

"You would have kissed him. You kiss the pizza guy, for God's sake."

I close my eyes and imagine that very first moment when I laid eyes on Seb. Despite the potential for calamity, I would have definitely kissed him, possibly more if I'm being completely honest with myself. "He didn't exactly roll with the punches, laugh off the calamities, and take me into his arms under the pouring rain. Nope. He even refused my invitation to buy something sweet at Pies Before Guys. Not exactly a rom-com moment. In fact, he'd rather watch The Shining over When Harry Met Sally. A clear sign he could be an axe murderer after all."

Junie sets her cookie down and studies me with her keen psychologist's eyes. "Okay, so the date may have been a bust, and he seems like a little bit of a jerk, but surely something good happened today."

My heart beats faster as excitement bubbles up inside me. "Actually, yes. Among all the comedic tragedies of this evening, I received some fantastic news."

"Amazing!" Junie gives me a high five.

I shift positions, tucking my feet under my butt. "I landed a job at Innovative Advertising."

Junie's eyes widen in surprise. "That's incredible! What's your objective? It can't be money."

"No," I confirm.

Money has never been my ultimate goal. It's just one means of measuring professional success. While my designs may be featured on every page of the Love Bug app, I don't believe they are the reason behind its massive success. Sure, they're cute, but the unique algorithm and clever questioning system Junie devised that seamlessly matches individuals together makes it a raging hit.

"What's next?"

"I don't want to be a one-hit wonder. I want to leave my mark on the advertising world. It would be great to come up with the next Nike swoosh, golden arches, or siren for a famous coffee company."

Junie chuckles and tucks a strand of hair behind her ear. "Liv, as great as our algorithm is at matching people, don't underestimate the power of those cute bugs. Especially that ladybug with heart wings. The branding and vibe are key factors in setting the tone before users even answer their first question."

I look away, experiencing a sudden weight in my chest. "I just want to create something iconic, instantly recognized everywhere. I want to achieve success on my own merits and have it recognized."

She reaches over and squeezes my hand. "You've already started with Love Bug. Your visuals and design are essential to our brand's identity. The app wouldn't have the same charm without your touch. They are just as crucial to our success as the matching questions."

My heart warms slightly. "Thanks, Junie. It's just ... difficult sometimes. It's like everything I have, every accomplishment, is built upon someone else's idea. I want to do something unrelated to my family's wealth or name. I need to create something truly original."

"And you think you'll achieve that by working for someone else?"

I pause, nibbling on my bottom lip nervously. "I believe working there could bring new opportunities, and valuable experiences, and help me hone my skills. Maybe, just maybe, it'll ignite that one brilliant idea within me. Besides, I can't go through life as a lone warrior at work too."

Junie leans back, her gaze piercing yet contemplative. "Sometimes, venturing out of our comfort zones and immersing ourselves in different environments can be magical. Look at what happened to me when I had to represent the app in The Great App Challenge. But remember, it's not just about where you are, but who you are. Your essence and perspective will add a unique touch to whatever you do."

I shake my head. "You always know how to make me feel both reassured and uncertain simultaneously."

She smirks. "It's a gift. But seriously, no matter which path you choose, remember you're not alone on the journey. Innovative Advertising seems like a great next stop. Can't do better than that for ad agencies. They've won a lot of awards for creative work."

"Thanks, my friend. I feel particularly good because they're taking me on as an Art Director, a step above Graphic Artist. That role gives me some creative strategy responsibility too. I won't be just an artist who executes someone else's ideas. That was important to me. It's also the only way they could justify a salary that would make it worth my while given all the royalties I get for Love Bug. I'll be forever grateful to you for taking a chance on me."

"You were the only choice." She picks up the remote and smiles. "And now for the important decision, *50 First Dates,* or *How to Lose a Guy in 10 Days?*"

I chuckle. "To be honest, I'm skilled in both areas. Hey, I lost a guy in ten minutes tonight. But I'm truly searching for a strong, meaningful connection."

"Oh!" Junie snaps her fingers. "You're talking about finding a *Serendipity* kind of connection! Like fate and destiny and all that?"

I nod. "Exactly."

"Well," Junie says, tilting her head and raising an eyebrow. "Perhaps it's time to give Love Bug another chance? Maybe you'll find your soulmate."

Internally, I struggle with the idea. I had deleted the dating app because even though I matched with a lot of interesting looking guys, no one felt like the right fit. It was like finding one specific grain of sand on a vast beach. If the app couldn't find a suitable match for one of its creators, did it really work?

Junie tilts her head and taps her finger against her lips, lost in thought. "You know, Liv, have you ever considered that you match with so many people because of how you answered the questions? You exude positivity and sunshine. You're practically a Pollyanna. Perhaps every answer you gave was just brimming with positivity."

I snort and cross my arms. "Are you saying I'm unrealistically optimistic?"

Junie's face lights up. "I'm suggesting that it's time to reassess those questions. Be completely honest this time.

Don't just give the correct, or positive answer. Real relationships are built on a wide range of genuine emotions, not just happy thoughts."

"Or wishful thinking apparently." I chew my bottom lip, mulling over her words. "But I truly believed in my answers when I first entered them into the app."

Junie lets out a sympathetic sigh and places a hand on my shoulder. "And that's okay. People change and grow. It's time for your answers to reflect who you are now, not who you were then."

I release a resigned breath. "Fine, I'll revisit the questions. But I'm holding you accountable if I become a moth instead of a butterfly."

Junie smirks. "Hey, moths have their own strengths. They're adaptable, and—"

"They're attracted to flames," I interject with a raised eyebrow.

She brushes off my comment with a wave of her hand. "Minor details. But don't worry, you'll still be our beautiful butterfly. Only with a touch more edge and reality mixed in."

I have to admit that Junie's push is appreciated. It's precisely what I need to truly find my perfect match. As *Serendipity* unfolds, I answer all the questions again and realize my perspective has changed on many.

I ponder one question in particular about persistence. *If, at first, you don't succeed, do you try, try again?* The saying plays on repeat in my mind, but then a burst of unexpected humor bursts out from within me as I consider—yes, unless it involves herpes or syphilis. For those situations, zero attempts are definitely preferred. I laugh at my joke and wonder when my sense of humor took this turn. Has it matured, or have I simply embraced a more lighthearted side of myself?

Taking a deep breath, I answer the app's questions again and hit enter. The screen goes blank before displaying a spinning ladybug with heart-shaped wings fluttering in what seems like a celebration. My heart races with anticipation. I know it's just an app, just a series of algorithms and lines of code, but it seems personal and exciting at this moment.

Gradually, the pixels on the screen shift and a dark figure with wings materializes. A sudden fear creeps in— have I transformed from a butterfly into a moth? Holding my breath, I hope and pray that the symbol of my identity remains unchanged. Finally, the image stabilizes, and there it is, the familiar red butterfly, vibrant and alive. My avatar. Me. Relief floods over me, mixed with a slight sense of disappointment and unmet expectations. Yes, my avatar stayed the same, but will the outcome be identical too?

CHAPTER FOUR

SEB

A thin beam of sunlight slips through the blinds, shining directly into my eyes like a harsh spotlight. No sweet-talking interrogators here, just the brutal truth of another morning. I reflect on my disappointing weekend and realize that if Ryan is the best date I can get, I may need to re-evaluate my approach to life as well as love.

The clock on my nightstand remains quiet, but I hear it ticking away in my head, each second a reminder of my recent mistakes and missteps. Ryan's words about compromise echo, but I push them aside.

I stretch out, the sheets resting on me like the residue of a night of poor decisions—without the fun. Flexibility, Ryan says? So, I'm not very flexible these days. My so-called flexibility had me bending over backward to please and take care of others until I cracked—like a contortionist with a bad back. The last time I gave someone my trust, they returned it shattered and worthless. When you lose, you adjust.

As I lay there surrounded by frustration and soft cotton sheets, I realize it's time for a change. Yet, as I recall my disastrous date with Olivia—her laughter, the way her eyes crinkled with genuine joy—I wonder if perhaps my heart's issue isn't about being too flexible but about not bending enough in the right direction.

After showering and getting dressed in my Monday suit—always gray, as if to remind myself of the dullness of corporate life—I'm ready for any obstacles that may come my way. As I go to the kitchen, I take out my phone and open the dating app, scrolling through it with disappointment at the empty notification bar. My friend Ryan is right. I'm too rigid and set in my ways. Perhaps I've been waiting for a perfect match that doesn't exist, like searching for a four-leaf clover in a field of wheat. It would be easy to see. It's just not there. It's time for me to step outside of my comfort zone, beyond the safety of solitude and the rules I've written to protect it. Perhaps what I need isn't a perfect match, but someone who challenges me and colors outside the lines of my carefully drawn life.

Forgoing my usual morning coffee, I head to work, determined to conquer the day. When I arrive, my assistant Jen informs me that our new hire, Liv Kato, will arrive soon. She is just what our company needs—a fresh perspective and a new approach. We are also down an art director, so there's that.

"When she arrives, have her come in."

I'm sitting at my desk, surrounded by papers and notes for the Soy Joy Cookies campaign. This isn't just another project. It's our lifeline. If we secure this contract, Innovative Advertising will stay afloat. But if we lose to my ex-partner and his flashy new firm, it's not just another blow to my pride. We need more momentum to keep growing or eventually, the client list will contract, and it would be game over for us.

To make matters worse, the campaign is all about vegan cookies. If I had only paid more attention to Olivia's interest in plant-based cuisine during our disastrous date, she might have had valuable insights that would be helpful right now. Instead, here I am, struggling to figure out how to sell a product I know nothing about in order to save my teetering company.

A knock on the door interrupts my thoughts. It opens, and Jen announces that the new hire is here. When Jen moves aside, Olivia stands there as if I had summoned her. It's the most surprising thing that has happened to me since she lit the restaurant on fire.

"Wow, this is unreal," I mutter.

She enters the room, and instantly, everything is charged, as if an electric current is running through every molecule. My heart races with either anticipation or dread—I can't tell which yet. Liv, short for Olivia. I would have never thought to call her that.

Against the muted shades in my office, she stands out like a vibrant painting. Her blouse is the color of a clear summer sky, and her tailored suit exudes competence and sophistication. With just her presence, she commands attention effortlessly. Unlike our previous encounter at a dimly lit restaurant, she shines under the harsh fluorescent lights here. There's an air of grace about her, even as she stands awkwardly with a half-smile on her lips, torn between extending a hand or fleeing. Considering how our last interaction ended, I wouldn't blame her for choosing the latter.

"What are the chances?" she muses.

Jen interrupts our moment, asking if we know each other.

Olivia recovers quickly, putting on a professional front. "We've crossed paths," she responds calmly. However, beneath her polished exterior, there's a hint of nervousness that wasn't there during our dinner date.

I stand there, attempting to form a coherent sentence that doesn't sound like it's been chopped by a paper shredder. "Yeah, it's a small world," I say with some effort, my voice sounding surprisingly composed given the current situation. The air is filled with questions and unsaid words, and I can sense Jen's curiosity growing. But she just nods, maintaining professionalism as her gaze shifts back to Olivia.

"Would you like some coffee?" she asks.

I look at Olivia, who shakes her head no. "That will be all for now," I tell Jen as she exits the room, leaving us in an awkward bubble of silence. Clearing my throat, I steer the conversation into more professional territory. "So, do you prefer Liv or Olivia?"

She replies, "Liv is fine. And S.E. Blackthorne translates into Seb?"

"It's my initials and also short for Sebastian."

She nods.

"Have a seat, Liv."

She walks to the front of my desk and sits in the first of the two chairs there.

"So, you're the new art director hired for the team?"

"It would appear so," she says, the steadiness in her voice wavering. "Unless, of course, you don't think I'm a good fit based on our brief encounter," she adds nervously as she catches her lower lip between her teeth.

Despite my usual steadfast corporate persona, I experience a flicker of empathy for her vulnerability. I quickly reassure her that our personal incident will not affect her job at this company. Wanting to put her at ease, I ask about her biggest accomplishment in her career so far. Although I know she has worked on a major successful app, the details have eluded me.

"Am I being interviewed again?"

She seems to be back to thinking she didn't get the job. "My team assures me you are more than qualified, a real talent, and I'm very happy to have you. I am just curious about your proudest moment," I clarify.

She reaches into her satchel and pulls out a folder, sliding it toward me on the desk. "This is my most recent work, but it does not fully showcase my capabilities. My proudest achievement was getting hired at Innovative Advertising. Even though my position is part art director, part graphic designer, I am determined to make a strong impression." Her cheeks flush with embarrassment. "I mean, a different impression than the one I made the other night."

Based on our previous encounter, I expect the

woman to be a walking disaster. However, her words resonate with me. She is most proud of being hired by my team. This brings me a sense of satisfaction, despite my conflicting emotions. "Again, we are fortunate to have you," I sincerely say, though I'm still navigating the dual roles of Seb-the-boss and Seb-the-terrible-date. "Should I have the fire department on alert?" My attempt to lighten the moment is about as welcome as the fire sprinklers at dinner.

I open the folder she hands me and find designs for the dating app I've been toying with. It's filled with animated bugs of various types and incredibly clever. The irony is not lost on me. Just as I am about to discuss her work, a notification from the app pops up on my phone. I have a match—a butterfly. A stag beetle and a butterfly—there must be some metaphor there about transformation and unexpected connections, but it eludes me for now.

There's no time for distractions. I focus on the task and the work that needs my attention. Yet, as I look up at Liv, the unspoken hangs between us. The elephant in the room needs addressing.

"About the other night," I begin, tipping my head toward her, "let's agree to banish it from memory. It's good that it didn't work out, as we have a no-dating policy."

Surprisingly, she responds with a laugh. "I couldn't agree more. We've seen enough commotion to last a lifetime. Besides, I want to earn my place here, not be given it because I was dating the boss."

Relieved that she's willing to let it go, my curiosity

gets the best of me. "Why go on a blind date when you helped create the hottest dating app?"

She shrugs. "Sometimes you have to trust a friend of a friend of a friend, you know? It seemed more personal than relying on a machine's algorithm."

I nod in agreement. "Welcome aboard," I say, closing her folder and handing it back to her. The contents are full of potential, promising what she could bring to our team. Standing up from my desk, I walk her to the door. "Jen will show you to the Creative Department. We have a new project that seems tailor-made for you." I shake my head slightly. "It's just a coincidence. Best of luck to you. I'm looking forward to great things from you."

As she walks away, a sway in her step seems to echo through the stillness of the office, leaving a trail of what-ifs and maybes. I wish her luck, but it's not hers I'm now questioning. It's mine. What were the chances of meeting her again, let alone as our crucial new hire?

I walk back to my desk and slump into my chair, the ghost of her perfume lingering like a whispered secret. I remind myself that there's a match waiting on Love Bug that isn't Liv. I've done the friend of a friend dance and look where that got me. It's time to let the algorithms and machines take the wheel. After all, what's the worst that could happen? I open the app and see my first challenge.

What's the most ridiculous way you've ever impressed a date, and what did you learn from it?

My mind goes straight to the date with Liv, but I

refuse to describe it scene by scene out of respect for Liv and damage control to my ego. So, I change it and make it more about the menu than the mishap.

Once, I tried to impress a date by confidently ordering the entire tasting menu, thinking variety was the spice of life. The spice was five-alarm-fire-station-on-speed-dial level. Who knew culinary bravery could be like a five-course inferno and end up needing an extinguisher. What I learned was to always ask questions and never, ever let your pride order for you. Because sometimes, the real test isn't on the plate, it's in the humbling realization shared over coughs and desperate sips of water that perhaps I don't always know best.

CHAPTER FIVE

LIV

As Jen ushers me through the gleaming halls of
Innovative Advertising, I feel like a new kid being
paraded around on the first day of school. She's like one
of those tour guides who's walked the path so many times
she could do it blindfolded—and probably backward.

"And this is the pit," Jen announces with a sweeping
gesture encompassing an open space buzzing with activity. It's a jungle of cubicles, with ethernet cables swinging
from desk to desk instead of vines.

"At the heart of the chaos stands Tom, our data
analyst," she says. The balding man is surrounded by
monitors that blink at him like he's the commander of a
spaceship. "Tom can predict client behavior better than a
fortune teller at a county fair," Jen says, and Tom gives a
salute that's more Star Trek than Army.

"Next up is Leena, our social media maestro." She is
an attractive blonde wearing headphones and bobbing to
the beat of whatever she's listening to. "She's got more

followers than a video post of a Super Bowl half-time nip-slip," Jen says. "And I swear Leena's fingers fly over the keyboard at the speed of light—tweeting, posting, hash-tagging into infinity."

We weave through the maze, Jen pointing out the heartbeats of the office. "Here's the Want Wall," she says, gesturing to a bulletin board plastered with everything from concert tickets to pleas for plant sitters. It's a tapestry of desires, each post-it a window into the soul of my new coworkers.

Then, the pièce de résistance—the lunchroom. It's a cornucopia of every dietary trend known to mankind, with a snack bar that boasts more nuts than a squirrel's paradise. "You are welcome to share a joke," Jen says, gesturing toward a wall adorned with cartoon strips and clever wordplay that is delightfully terrible. "Laughter's the second-best medicine here. The first is coffee."

The tour continues, and she shows me the gym where treadmills face TVs running ads on a loop. "For inspiration—or to run away from bad ideas," Jen jests, and I make a mental note to bring gym clothes ... or a pillow because apparently, there's also a nap room.

"It's for creative recharging," Jen explains, but I can't shake the feeling that it's less about recharging and more about never leaving. The room has a better ambiance than my apartment, complete with soothing sounds and mood lighting.

"Do people ever go home here?" I ask, half-joking.

Jen winks. "Why go home when you've got all this?"

Her arms sweep over the space like she's showing off a wonder of the world. And honestly, it's not far off.

I'm thinking I've landed a gig in some sort of corporate Narnia—just waiting for a lion to pop up. But until then, I've got Jen, queen of the realm, leading me through the enchanted forest of office life.

Jen's voice lowers to a hush as we round the last corner. "And there's Vicky, our Creative Director, your boss. She's also new to her position." She breathes out. Vicky strides toward us, each step deliberate, her heels clicking out an authoritative cadence on the tile. She radiates a blend of runway elegance and corporate power, her gaze cutting through the office buzz. A knowing smile curls on her lips as if she's privy to every secret these walls hold. "I think the step up from your role to hers might have deprived her of oxygen and made her light-headed. Vicky thinks she's in charge," Jen mutters under her breath. "Of everyone and everything."

"Looks like she is," I respond, noticing how all eyes are on her and how the bustling atmosphere quiets down as she passes. Vicky gives off a vibe that she can assess your value with a single glance and dismantle any argument with a flick of her perfectly manicured hand.

I pull my jacket tighter around me, suddenly aware of every wrinkle and crease in my outfit. My mother's words ring in my ears. "Dress for the day destiny comes knocking on your door." Well, destiny is here now, dressed to the nines.

"You must be Liv," Vicky greets me, her voice a blend of velvet and vigor.

"Yes, I am," I reply confidently.

"I heard you designed the Love Bug art. It's all so adorable," she says, thoughtfully placing a finger on her chin. "I even thought about what my avatar would be if I used the app."

I'm used to people asking me about their avatars. "What would it be?" I ask her curiously.

She shrugs. "Definitely a scorpion."

I'm familiar with the attributes after the hours of late-night chat sessions Junie and I had while she was putting together the list of avatars. "Oh, passionate, mysterious, resilient."

Vicky nods. "Yes, and I have no fear of striking when I'm backed into a corner." She waves her hand in the air. "But that's not why you're here. Our new campaign needs your touch. It's a campaign for Soy Joy cookies, and they are the focus."

"Do you think you can bring home the tofu?" Jen asks me, looking from Vicky to me.

"Would you like it steamed, deep fried, or baked?" I answer.

Vicky's piercing green eyes, which match the color of her blouse, lock onto me. They're not an ordinary shade of green. They're like a traffic light daring me to hit the gas or slam on the brakes. And by the slight arch of her perfectly shaped eyebrow, I know it's time to go full speed ahead.

"I'm ready to give it my best shot."

"Good," she says firmly. "We have a pitch due soon, and I want fresh, bold, and brilliant ideas. Make them believe that eating Soy Joy is like experiencing a second coming of cookies." With a sly smile, she adds, "Even though they taste like sawdust. They'd be so much better if they used butter."

I could be offended by her remark and point out that butter is not vegan, but I decide against it. Instead, I simply nod and let my mind generate ideas.

"I'm on board," I declare confidently.

Vicky nods in approval. "Fantastic. Remember, we're not just selling cookies. We're selling a lifestyle, even if it's a fabricated one. That's our job in advertising—to convince people to buy into our lies."

"I quite enjoy Soy Joy cookies," I state defiantly, thinking almost out loud that Vicky's description of what they do at Innovative Advertising seemed more than a little cynical, even coarse. "But my favorite is Pies Before Guys chocolate chip."

"To each their own. You'll find a folder with my slogan suggestions on your desk. I'll need some mock-ups from you by the end of the week. Feel free to do your own research and of course brainstorm with the other art directors if you must," As she walks away, my mind races with possibilities. It's time to get to work, to fully immerse myself in the world of Soy Joy. The challenge has been set before me.

I settle into my new desk, its minimalistic design complemented by an ergonomic chair that embraces my back with a reassuring hug. On the desk sits a folder filled with papers that offer glimpses into Soy Joy's world. With each slogan I read, my heart sinks a little. "Go vegan or go home." I raise an eyebrow in skepticism. Are we promoting a lifestyle or issuing ultimatums? The following slogan is no better. "Feed it, don't eat it!" I can barely stifle a groan. It's like they were written by a child.

As a new team member, I know that one misstep could result in being an outcast before my first concept board. But staying quiet would be like watching a disaster unfold and doing nothing to stop it. If this campaign fails, they will whisper about me behind closed doors. Taking a deep breath, I lean back and chew on my pen as I look at the poorly thought-out slogans. "Creamy Dreams" and "Cheese the Day" may be catchy, but they are misleading for a vegan campaign. The pressure is on, and I can practically feel the team's collective gaze on my neck.

I refuse to crack under the stress, so I grab a notepad as a signal that taking risks is just part of the job, but I have to do it my way. These generic slogans don't align with my perspective on veganism.

Quickly jotting down ideas, a few slogans come to mind. "Savor the Soy," "Purely Plant-Powered," and "Bean Bliss." They're straightforward, bold, and unapologetically vegan. It's better to stay true to the brand's values than to get lost in a sea of conflicting messages.

Nestled in my cozy corner, the soft light of my computer screen illuminates me as I come up with slogan after slogan. "Seeds of Change." "Savor the Soysation." Each is like a minor rebellion against what's been handed to me.

As I scratch out another rejected option and replace it with "Immerse Yourself in Pure, Plant-Powered Pleasure," I wonder if I'm creating slogans or mantras to survive in this environment.

The clock ticks slowly, and the office noise fades into silence as people head home for the day. In this peaceful moment, I sense his presence before I even see him—Seb, casually leaning against the frame of my cubicle.

"Working your magic, I presume?" His tone is teasing, but his eyes scan the pile of discarded dairy-related slogans covering my desk.

I offer a half-smile, feeling validated in my choices. "I'm just steering the Soy Joy ship away from crashing against the dairy aisle."

He picks up one of the rejected lines and raises an eyebrow. "Milk's favorite cookie? That's not exactly on point." His expression turns serious as he asks, "Did Vicky give you this?"

"Yeah, but I don't think we're targeting the "got milk?" audience," I reply confidently, meeting his gaze. "I know I'm supposed to illustrate something representing the slogan, but I don't want to waste everyone's time and resources with something that won't sell."

Seb nods in agreement. "You're right. We want to be the almond milk's perfect match, not just a sidekick to the dairy industry. Our target audience isn't meat eaters who might enjoy vegan cookies. It's people like you. Your input is crucial for us to win this campaign. The market is large and growing,"

His validation is like a shot of caffeine after a long day. It's good to be seen and heard.

As I mentally congratulate myself for the clever soy

puns, Vicky strides through the office with her signature confident yet slightly predatory walk.

Seb looks at the stack of slogans, a slight frown creasing his forehead. "Vicky," he says calmly, "these Soy Joy themes don't seem to align with our vegan message. Would you agree?"

She steps back as if pushed, but no one has touched her. "Just a little test for Liv," she replies, her voice sharp like a knife's edge. "I wanted to see if she would catch the ... inconsistencies."

"Oh, thank goodness," I say. "I was afraid these were serious slogans about using milk and cheese in vegan products." Relief floods me until I catch something flickering in Vicky's eyes—anger? It disappears quickly and is replaced by a smoldering gaze for Seb.

"So, we're keeping it dairy-free and dreamy?" she purrs and reaches out to slide her hand down Seb's arm. It's so seductive that I wonder if something is going on between them, making me wonder if his no-dating policy is real and if we're not back in 1959 again. Maybe she missed the diversity and inclusion training module about sexual harassment prevention. It goes both ways.

But Seb immediately steps back as if he's been shocked. Either he took the class, or he genuinely doesn't like being stroked by her like he's a sleeping kitten.

With a false sense of conviction, I let out a forced declaration. "I'm relieved that I passed the test. I'll get to work if you can provide me with the real tag lines and other copy that's been written. Is there a market research folder, notes from strategy sessions?" I gather some slogans I came up with and hand them over to Vicky. "You might consider some of these instead. They resonate a bit more with the target audience I believe."

Seb nods in approval, breaking the tension in the room. "Great, stay vigilant," he advises before turning to Vicky. "There's no time for trial runs. Our success hinges on securing this account." He exits the room without another word.

As Seb's footsteps fade away, Vicky's demeanor changes completely. Her friendly facade drops as her eyes narrow, and her voice becomes threatening. "What are you playing at, Liv?" she demands. "You don't get to take everything that's mine on your first day. If I were you, I'd watch my back. This is an environment full of sharks, not dolphins. And trying to drag your manager into dangerous waters? That's a risky move you might regret."

Her words shiver down my spine, unrelated to the chilly office temperature. It's a warning from someone who knows how to wield their power and is daring me to step out of line.

"I wasn't trying to—"

Vicky's heels echo loudly on the tiled floor as she turns and walks away. I let out a breath I didn't even realize I was holding and reach for my bag, eager to leave. As I join the crowd of coworkers making their way out, my phone buzzes with a notification from Love Bug—I've been matched with someone. My heart races as the image of a stag beetle appears on the screen against a white backdrop. Intrigued, I stop in my tracks to read the prompt. According to the app, the stag beetle represents strength and determination, and is often associated with leadership and resilience.

As I face off against a self-proclaimed scorpion, I think about the rugged exterior of a beetle. In this situation, I'm more like a delicate butterfly. But that might not be bad. Perhaps my transformative nature will be helpful on this journey. These thoughts lead me to ponder how a stag beetle and a butterfly, two opposite creatures, could complement each other. The beetle's strength and strategy could stabilize the butterfly's adaptability and growth. It's an intriguing concept but doesn't immediately make sense to me. However, remembering Junie's words to trust the process, I consider her successful match with AJ and remind myself to give this a real chance. Just as I'm mulling over these ideas, another notification pops up from "Stag Beetle Guy," who has already answered a question he was given.

What's the most outrageous way you've ever attempted to impress a date, and what did you take away from it?

His response is an unfiltered retelling of a spicy escapade, and the humility he gained is like a soothing ointment after a day full of bruises. It's a small connection to a world outside of corporate politics. A chuckle slips out as I finish reading his story. Walking down the busy sidewalk, I stop to think about Stag Beetle Guy's culinary confession. Pulling out my phone again, I type up a response—something that the app now allows—just one reply to his daring tale.

Your experience with the fiery-tasting menu takes courage and humor to another level. And who would have thought that humility could be such a refreshing palate cleanser? But let's be honest, the best stories always have a little spice in them.

I tap the "send" button on my phone, and a silly idea crosses my mind. *Could Mr. Stag Beetle be Seb in disguise?* I quickly brush off the thought with a snort and a head shake. I might have believed it if his answer included an impromptu indoor shower and a love for flaming table-side displays. But no, my fiery fiasco of a date? That was a different hot mess, not covered in spice.

Shaking off the nostalgia, my phone buzzes again with my question.

What has been your most unexpected challenge? It doesn't take long for the words to form in my head, a response crafted from the day's trials.

The most unexpected challenge? Let's just say it involved jumping into the deep end on my first day of trying something new and learning to navigate the waters where the current is fierce. But instead of floundering, I found my stroke.

I flag down a taxi and collapse into the rear seat. Before the driver can inquire, I quickly recite the address with the exhaustion of a soldier fleeing war. We barely make it one city block before my phone vibrates with a message from Junie.

How was your first day? The message on the screen gleams.

My fingers hover over the keyboard. If only sarcasm could travel through SMS.

Oh, fantastic, I type back, the words dripping with enough irony to stain the screen. **Just the usual—avoiding metaphorical bullets, navigating office politics, and narrowly escaping being sacrificed to the vegan cookie gods. #Living-TheDream**

I hit send as the taxi navigates through traffic as smoothly as I handled professional pitfalls today. Hopefully, Junie will catch onto my snark ... or perhaps she'll assume I'm up for a promotion. Knowing my luck today, she'll probably send a congratulatory fruit basket to my apartment.

Is an emergency girls' night needed? She fires back. It's the virtual equivalent of a comforting arm around my shoulders.

Rain check, I reply. **Dinner at Mom and Dad's.**

Is that wise?

Wise? No choice, you know, it's required. Guess what?

What?

My new boss is Seb.

There's a long pause.

No way! That can't be a coincidence.

It is, and if it wasn't, it wouldn't matter. Because he doesn't date employees.

That's a stupid policy.

I don't know. It's likely a good idea in my case. Talk soon.

I put my phone away and challenge the universe, daring it to throw whatever it wants my way. Part of me hopes it will decline the invitation. However, as I reach my parents' house, a nagging sensation makes me think that this day isn't done with me just yet.

CHAPTER SIX

SEB

Heading back to my quiet office, I can't shake off the image of Liv and Vicky's confrontation. It was like watching a newcomer go up against an experienced pro, but Liv held her ground in the most diplomatic of ways. I'm realizing that she's more than just a pretty face. She's a valuable asset to our company. She's perceptive and has a great sense of the bigger picture, which our company needs.

I probably should have intervened when Vicky attacked her, but I was torn between wanting to protect Liv and wanting to witness the exchange. Besides, she gave me the distinct impression that she wanted to handle the situation herself. What I saw was someone who didn't need saving. She can hold her own and become a force to be reckoned with. Liv radiates with a passion that I haven't seen in years. It reminds me of my younger self before cynicism and caution became ingrained in me.

As the evening quiets down, I let out a laugh to myself. "Lit by fire," I say aloud, remembering Liv's fiery entrance on our date. But her flame isn't one of destruction. It has the potential to ignite something extraordinary. That's exactly what we need at Innovative Advertising—not a quick burst of excitement but a steady burn of everlasting creativity.

I lean back in my chair, crossing my arms behind my head and taking a moment to appreciate the ironic twist life has thrown at me. Of course, I'll keep an eye on Liv, but not because she might set everything on fire—though I'll have an extinguisher nearby, just in case. No, I'll watch her because she can set the advertising world ablaze, which I want to witness firsthand. She's idealistic but practical, talented, and daring, not jaded.

My train of thought is interrupted by a notification from the Love Bug app from my mysterious match, "Butterfly." She's responded to my answer about impressing a date, causing a happy reaction to cross my lips. Her wit is sharp, and her words are almost poetic.

With a simple question, she turns our conversation into a lively exchange, and a weight lifts off my shoulders. Having such a connection with a stranger is unexpected, a welcome break from the usual monotony of business negotiations and competitive tactics. I want to know more about her, to uncover the person hiding behind the virtual avatar. Another message pops up from Butterfly. She has been given a question to answer.

What has been your most unexpected challenge?

I read her answer. This girl seems fearless. I think about all the unexpected obstacles that have come my way recently, and my fingers hit the keyboard. I reply to her question, but not from a place of honesty or vulnerability.

The most unexpected challenge for me would be navigating my drive to work. It's like my personal version of Frogger or Donkey Kong, where I'm diving and dodging the entire way.

After sending the message, I lean back in my chair, my mind swirling with professional competition and personal relationships. It's a delicate balance, staying sharp in business while allowing myself to open up to potential personal connections.

Suddenly, the loud ringing of my phone breaks through my thoughts. I answer, trying to push aside any irritation lurking beneath the surface.

"Sebastian speaking."

"Seb, buddy," the voice of my former partner, Brad, fills my ear, oozing fake friendliness. It's hard to believe that I used to call him friend. He broke up the partnership and when I refused to liquidate the business, he transformed from friend to foe. "Just thought I'd give you a heads up. You know we're both vying for the Soy Joy campaign, and since I snagged the talent, you might as well surrender."

"Why would I do that?" I respond coolly, suppressing my annoyance.

He lets out a laugh that makes me cringe. It sounds like a hyena's screech, grating and piercing. "Because you're outmatched. I've seen your pitches, man. It's like watching a kitten try to be a lion."

My hand tightens into a fist as old feelings of betrayal resurface. "We'll see about that," I say sharply. "Innovation isn't just part of our company name—it's what sets us apart."

"And you think Vicky is your secret weapon? She's like a stale piece of bread pretending to be a gourmet croissant."

"I have new art direction talent on board now," I counter confidently. "She's creating quite the buzz in town. Bring your A-game."

"Oh, we will."

After ending the call, his laughter still echoes in my ear. I set the phone down, filled with a mix of fortitude and frustration. He's challenged me and my team, doubting our abilities. But I can't afford to doubt myself now. The success of my company is on the line, and I am ready for the challenge. It's not just about proving him wrong. It's about proving that I'm right.

I glance at my phone again as it goes dark. On reflection, the response I sent through the Love Bug app doesn't sit well with me. It seems fake, like something I'm supposed to say. Since my former partner left, taking half of what we had built together, including Mia —our creative design lead—and a portion of our staff,

I've built walls to protect myself. But now those walls are more like a fortress, keeping everything—good and bad—out.

He didn't just take our assets and leave. He also took away my trust, leaving me constantly guarded and wary. And that's why my response on the app feels fake. I'm trying to protect not just my business but also myself from getting too close to anyone again. I glance back at my phone, at the app that promises genuine connections, and I see a reflection of someone who has played it safe for far too long. My answer to Butterfly was shallow, lacking real depth or substance. This app is meant for honesty, yet I gave the most surface-level response possible. How can I hope to find something genuine if I can't even be true to myself?

Part of me wants to go back and rewrite my reply authentically, as the real me—not the ad exec, not the man with a heart made of stone. But the rules are clear. There's no "edit" button or chance for a do-over. Perhaps it's a sign that it's time to break down these walls I've built and let the truth out, in order to let someone in.

I pack up my belongings. The office is now quiet compared to the earlier hustle and bustle. My mind is a jumble of thoughts—the alluring messages from Butterfly, Liv's perceptive observations, and the lingering sting from my call with Brad. Each thought vies for attention, creating a tumultuous whirlwind in my head. I close my briefcase with a click and stand up, feeling a sense of closure despite the day's loose ends.

As I walk through the deserted office, the quiet is so

intense it almost echoes, completely different from the normal hustle and bustle.

Exiting the building, I go to my car and drive to my go-to spot for dinner. Having some peace and quiet after such a hectic day is a relief.

I follow the well-known streets, each turn bringing me closer to my haven of culinary delights. The Bistro, a cozy establishment I frequent enough to be considered a regular, welcomes me with its inviting ambiance and hushed conversations. I sink into my usual booth in a corner, a private nook that seems like an extension of my personal space. Here, the outside world fades away as I focus on the table before me, relishing in the sense of anonymity. The server, who knows me by now, acknowledges me with a nod and soon returns with a glass of rich buttery Chardonnay, its aroma hinting at a brief escape from reality.

I order my regular dish, grilled salmon, which has never disappointed me. While I wait for my food to arrive, my mind drifts back to Butterfly and our conversations. There's a sense of excitement and curiosity in trying to uncover the true identity beneath her online persona. I find it frustrating that I can't see her face, but that's just how this app works. The challenge is building a connection based on shared humor, inside jokes, and the anticipation of a meeting in person. It's like solving a puzzle in the dark, where each piece is an exchanged word or message, slowly revealing who she really is. This enigma is equal parts irritating and thrilling.

The dish is set in front of me, its aroma tantalizing my

taste buds before I take the first bite. The flavors burst onto my tongue, each forkful reminding me that there is still simplicity and joy to be found amidst the chaos. As I savor the salmon's texture and the wine's depth, the tension of the day slowly dissipates. For a moment, I am just a man enjoying a delicious meal, not a busy executive caught in an endless game of strategy. With each bite, my thoughts shift from today's struggles to tomorrow's possibilities. The vibrant and satisfying flavors on my palate reflect the potential I see in Liv's abilities and the budding connection with Butterfly. It reminds me that life may have moments of bitterness, but it offers its fair share of sweetness.

The drive home after dinner is almost routine, and I switch on the lamp as I enter my living room. The large window immediately catches my attention, and I settle into the comfortable chair beside it. The cityscape outside is a beautiful display of old-world charm and modern lights twinkling against the darkening sky. It's one reason I fell in love with this house. As I sit in silence, memories of the day play out in my mind. The surprise of Liv showing up as my new employee. The call from my former partner, meant to intimidate me, only strengthens my desire to approach the game differently. Success isn't just about winning at all costs. It's about how you play. This philosophy, ingrained in my company, is different from Brad's grab-and-go mentality, where he's willing to seize opportunities without concern for the aftermath.

Glancing at my phone, I see brief messages exchanged with Butterfly. It's a source of unexpected comfort, talking to someone who knows nothing of my world or battles.

As the night approaches, the city grows quieter, its pulse a murmur in the distance. My house stands amidst it all, a perfect blend of past and present, like a peaceful island in the craziness. It's my safe place, where I can escape from the madness of the outside world.

My gaze lands on the half-finished model ship resting on the nearby shelf. It reminds me of all the projects and passions I've left unfinished. In a way, it reflects the parts of my life that have been neglected in pursuit of success. The thought is sobering.

Sitting here in this quiet space, I am enveloped by solitude. I contemplate the trade-offs I've made—achieving success at the cost of personal relationships and experiences. Have I tilted the scale too far in one direction? But, what about the people whose livelihoods depend on my putting my company first? The clients who count on us all? How much room is there for more? I haven't cracked that code, or even really thought about it till now.

I allow the view to relax me, and my mind wanders. Tomorrow may be another day in the office, another day in the game. But for now, I take this moment to gaze out my window and imagine all that lies beyond the horizon.

CHAPTER SEVEN

LIV

The taxi moves effortlessly onto the familiar street, stopping in front of the elegant Victorian mansion nestled in the heart of Pacific Heights. Its regal structure stands tall against the dusky sky, beckoning me back to a world that is increasingly distant from my own. I take a deep breath, trying to shake off the stress of the day, and remind myself that this is still my home, even though it may seem worlds apart from my current reality.

I'm dressed in work attire—a sharp navy-blue suit that serves as my armor on the battlefield at Innovative Advertising. My hair has lost its morning bounce, and my makeup has long surrendered to the day's challenges. Not exactly the polished look you'd expect for a fancy dinner, but it's who I am—unfiltered, battle-weary, and far from the fresh-faced daughter they're used to seeing.

I step outside, my heels clicking on the cobblestone driveway. I pause momentarily, taking in the imposing home where expectations hang as heavily as the expensive drapes. There will be signs of happiness, but also an underlying sense of "we know what's best for you."

Inhaling the cool San Francisco air, I straighten my posture and climb the steps, preparing to play the role of the dutiful daughter—at least for tonight.

The front door swings open before I can knock, revealing Claudia, my parents' housekeeper, with a bright smile.

"Welcome back, Miss Olivia," she says, as if I've been gone for longer than a week.

"Hello. It's good to be home," I reply. All I want tonight are some cookies and a hot bath.

"Your parents are waiting for you," Claudia informs me.

"Thank you." I step inside and am immediately greeted by the rich scents of the chef's cooking and my mother's signature perfume—a blend of lavender and something exotic that is as commanding and elegant as she is. The chandelier above casts a warm golden light, adding to the formal atmosphere of our weekly family dinner. There's a distinct difference between the charged environment of my office and this polished palace of silver and crystal. As I hang my blazer on the coat stand, the shirt underneath suddenly is too stiff and constrictive in this opulent embrace of home. But this is the expected script for a family dinner night—a dance of appearances and expectations.

I enter the living room, where my dad's booming voice greets me. He sits by the window with his ever-present tablet nearby, but a newspaper in hand. His financial world may now be digital, but some habits die hard.

My father's eyes light up when he sees me, and he sets his paper on the nearby table. "Olivia, there you are!" he says with a warm smile that crinkles the corners of his eyes. "You look sharp as ever. Definitely my genes at work."

I roll my eyes, but my affection for him is undeniable. "Sure, Dad. Because the other seventy-five percent that's not Japanese is just along for the ride, right?"

He chuckles heartily, the sound filling the room and bouncing off the high ceilings. "Exactly! But let's keep that between us. We wouldn't want your mom to be left out." He winks slyly, referencing our long-standing family joke that the best part of me comes from my Japanese Kato heritage.

My mother enters from the next room, commanding and authoritative like a CEO but dressed like Debutant Barbie. "A suit for dinner, Liv?" she says disapprovingly, as if I've shown up in my pajamas.

"It's business chic, Mom," I say, sensing some of the day's stress dissipate in this familiar back-and-forth banter. "Ever heard of it? Plus, it's a Dolce and Gabbana, and you bought it."

She gives me a thorough check with her practiced eye, circling around me before giving a nod of approval. "You have a talent for pulling it off, and I have impeccable taste, but don't forget that this isn't a board meeting. We dress for the occasion here." As my mom links arms with me and guides me toward the grand dining hall, I wonder, what is the dress code for vegan lasagna? Do I need to wear an evening gown or a cocktail dress? Maybe a diamond bib from Harry Winston? The thought almost makes me burst out laughing.

"Don't worry, Mom. Dressing appropriately is practically our family motto," I say with a hint of sarcasm, internally rolling my eyes. "So, what's the suggested outfit for tonight? Should I have brought my tiara, or would that be too much?"

Mom gently squeezes my arm, her eyes twinkling with humor. "Now, now, Liv. Let's not be dramatic. Although a tiara wouldn't be entirely out of place. I love the way they look."

"You appreciate the way they sparkle," I say. "Next time, I'll accessorize accordingly, and add some elbow-length gloves for good measure."

Mom laughs, a sound that's both melodious and a tad rehearsed. "Be yourself, Olivia. That's all we ask." The words feel like a costume that doesn't fit.

I smile, knowing full well that "being myself" is a relative term in this household. As we move to join Dad, who's already making his way to his usual spot at the head of the table, it's like I'm straddling two worlds—one where I'm Liv, the tech-savvy graphic designer, now one of many Art Directors at a prestigious agency, and another where I'm Olivia, the heiress to a legacy that still confuses a successful app with a fad. Each dinner feels like a quiet battle.

"Your father and I were discussing the charity ball a week from Saturday. You will attend, won't you?" It's a command veiled as a question, but my attendance is not up for debate.

I nod, already crafting mental notes to prepare for an evening of glitz I'd rather trade for a quiet night with a good book. But this is the world I come from, where dinner is never just dinner, and every gathering is a gala in disguise.

We walk through the opulent dining room, and Mom suddenly stops. Her eyes light up with excitement, like a fashionista who has just remembered a sale. "I have something for you before we sit down," she says, guiding me toward a box on a nearby table. It's no ordinary box. It exudes extravagance, adorned with silk paper that seems to whisper of luxury and exclusivity. Curious, I raise an eyebrow—Mom's gifts are always carefully chosen and make a statement.

With a flick of her wrist, she reveals the box's contents. Inside is a dress so stunning it appears to have been woven from the night sky itself. The fabric glimmers with elegance, clearly crafted by a top designer. The cut is so impeccable it could only have been tailored by magical creatures. "This will be perfect for your next event," Mom exclaims, her voice full of excitement and anticipation.

I run my fingers over the fabric in awe of its beauty. "It's stunning, Mom. But isn't it extravagant for a family dinner?" I say teasingly.

Mom's laughter rings airy and bright, yet her gaze holds an unspoken resolve. "Olivia, every occasion is an opportunity to showcase your best self. And your best self," she adds with a pointed stare, "wears nothing less than couture."

I laugh, placing the dress back into its shrine of a box. "I'll remember that next time I'm at a vegan lasagna summit."

Mom shakes her head, but I notice a hint of amusement in her expression. "You can wear it to the charity event."

"I will," I say, and I mean it. Because, despite the differences between my world and hers, I know this is how she shows love. Through stitches and seams, patterns, and palettes, she's weaving her hopes for me into every garment she chooses. And for tonight, that's enough to create a sense of being dressed in more than just silk and sequins—it's like being covered by my mother's love. I can control what I put in my body, but what's on it is woven with many things like silk and leather that my inner vegan would like to reject, but to do that would be to reject my mother's main love language. We all make compromises I remind myself. I can still be a vegan and wear silk, sort of.

We make our way to the table, a perfect picture of elegance and luxury. The silverware sparkles beneath the crystal chandelier and the China plates look too delicate to touch. Chef Andre, a master of culinary artistry, presents each dish with a theatrical flair, from the refreshing salad to the rich lasagna, to the warm bread drizzled with fragrant olive oil and herbs.

As we take our seats, Dad enthusiastically shares his latest stock market adventures, his voice filled with a passion for numbers and trends. Mom adds updates from her busy social calendar, gushing about upcoming galas and charity events like a seasoned socialite.

I try to squeeze in a word, eager to share the adventure of my first day at Innovative Advertising. "You won't believe the day I've had," I start, but Mom has already changed course.

"That's nice, dear, but have you given any more thought to that charming young man from the Hendersons' party? A match like that could set you up for life," she says, her eyes shimmering at the thought of a union that's more a business deal than marriage. "I was going to suggest meeting him at La Lumiére, but I heard some silly girl set it on fire the other night."

Shock jolts through me. "A fire? At La Lumiére?" I exclaim, pretending to be surprised with all the innocence I can muster. My heart races as I pretend to be clueless. "Wow, that's crazy! Surely it was just superficial. No one hurt?" I add a carefree laugh, not willing to share my role in the disaster with my parents, who don't need another reason to disapprove of me.

Growing weary of the small talk, Dad unknowingly steps in to save me. "How's the new job? Are you still making waves in the tech world?" he asks, genuinely interested.

I pause, unsure if I should open up about everything or keep it brief to avoid ruining the night. "It was my first day, so there were definitely some challenges. But that's where I excel—overcoming obstacles."

He nods and says, "That's my daughter. Always

reaching for the stars. Just remember, whatever you do, make sure it has meaning."

I grin, grateful for his support, even though he doesn't fully grasp the current demands of my "meaningful" work. It's comforting to have someone at the table who understands, even if they aren't privy to all the details.

As the conversation switches to safer topics, I pick at my food, my thoughts consumed by my work at Innovative. Part of me is still there, strategizing and navigating through uncharted territory. And in that reverie, I crave another dose of Seb's infectious encouragement—fueling my ambition and turning impossibilities into dares waiting to be conquered.

As dinner continues, the conversation lightens, and my parents share their own tales of "office drama," although theirs are far different from what I've experienced.

Dad's voice is laced with amusement as he tells his story. "You wouldn't believe what happened at the investment meeting," he says. "Harrison showed up wearing two different colored socks! It caused quite a stir."

I stifle a laugh, already picturing the scene in my mind. In Dad's world, mismatched socks are a significant crisis. "Oh, the horror," I reply, trying to keep a straight face. "How did you ever recover from such a catastrophe?"

Mom joins in on the fun, adding her own anecdote. "And at the charity auction, Mrs. Fletcher accidentally bid on the wrong lot. She donated ten thousand dollars for a gardening session instead of the wine-tasting tour she wanted in Napa. Needless to say, she was not happy."

I chuckle at the thought. "That's one expensive lesson in gardening. Did she at least get to keep the plants?"

Their laughter fills the room, a moment of pure joy that I treasure. These carefree moments in our dining room provide a sense of safety and calmness, very different from my professional world. Someday, I worry they might find me dead. With one of Vicky's stilettos plunged into my back. That woman seems from another time. Who behaves like that? I guess we are not all sisters breaking through the glass ceiling together after all, at least not with Vicky in the room.

After dinner and the last dessert crumbs are gone, my parents suggest moving to the living room for coffee and brandy. It's a smooth transition, a well-rehearsed part of our evening ritual. We sink back into the comfortable sofas as antique lamps cast a soft light around us, creating shadows on the walls.

Dad pours the brandy effortlessly while the rich aroma mixes with the scent of fresh coffee. Their conversation resumes effortlessly, filled with teasing banter and continual laughter. I lean back, letting their voices wash over me.

As the night winds down, I gather my courage to bridge the gap between our worlds. "I think my boss might hate me," I say hesitantly, attempting to steer the conversation toward something more relatable to my daily life.

"Don't be ridiculous. No one dislikes you," my mom insists before changing the subject. "And Olivia, you must attend the next party at the Hendersons'. It's going to be the highlight of the entire season." There is a slight sting of disappointment to being invisible in my home. But I push it away, accepting this is how things are. I am present but not truly seen. My dreams and accomplishments are mere murmurs in the grand narrative of their lives where I will eventually marry well, and they will no longer need to worry about me. As I say goodnight and receive their usual warm hugs and kisses, I experience a twinge of yearning—for recognition, understanding, and a deeper connection. But for now, I am content to let the evening end on its familiar note. As I leave with my new dress, my mother pulls me aside for one last word. "Remember, Olivia," she says firmly, locking her gaze onto mine with that unwavering intensity that is part matriarch and part mentor. "You are destined for great things."

Her faith in me warms my heart, even if her definition of success differs significantly from mine. "I know, Mom." Although she may hope for me to climb the social ladder, her words only strengthen my resolve to make my mark. In my world, achieving great things means making a name for myself at Innovative Advertising rather than marrying into wealth. I hug her, embracing the familiar scent of her perfume that reminds me of my past life but also remains a part of who I am. "Goodnight, Mom." As I step out into the evening, I see the car my father arranged waiting for me. The cool air on my skin chills me as the grandeur of the mansion fades into the background.

As the car moves through the peaceful streets of Pacific Heights, I stare out the window and admire the sparkling city lights. They bring me back to reality, but my mind is already racing with thoughts of upcoming projects, strategies to be devised, and creative obstacles to overcome. A sense of exhilaration comes from chasing after what truly ignites my passion. My chosen path awaits me ahead, promising great things as I continue to pursue my dreams.

Just as I arrive home, my phone buzzes with a notification from the Love Bug app.

Field Trip Challenge: Explore the Japanese Tea Gardens and who knows? Maybe you'll find love blooming among the cherry blossoms.

I quickly check the date—Saturday. With nothing on my calendar, I hit "accept." Worst-case scenario, I indulge in some cookies and tea.

CHAPTER EIGHT

SEB

A soft chime from my phone snags my attention, a new alert lighting up the screen— **Field Trip Challenge: Explore the Japanese Tea Gardens, and who knows? Maybe you'll find love blooming among the cherry blossoms.**

I lean back in my desk chair while my thumb hovers and hesitates. Who is this enigma with the butterfly avatar? I wonder if she shares Liv's serene composure, the kind that allowed her to laugh with lightness amidst the licking flames of our only date.

Liv… She possesses a certain allure that's hard to ignore. Amidst the chaos of the restaurant that night, her sense of humor soared—untouched and genuine. And, when I, in a moment of defeat, suggested we cut our losses, she simply agreed, no offense taken. What did I have to lose by going to the bakery with her? Why didn't I just say yes instead of watching her walk away? What was I afraid of? Vegan cookies? The irony of that question is not lost on me given the Soy Joy account we need to land.

There's something about her, this undeniable spark that has me tossing and turning at night, replaying every smile, every casual touch on a loop in my mind. It's ludicrous to be this wound up over someone who's now just a name on my payroll. Yet, here I am, etching that line in the sand so deep it might as well be a trench because I refuse to cross it. I've witnessed the chaos of mixing business with pleasure, how it tangles up your priorities until you can't tell your heart from your head. The opportunity for drama working with mostly creative people is already exceptionally high. Add romance and you have a tinder keg.

Brad is a prime example. He fell head over heels for another graphic artist named Mia and lost sight of the empire we built from scratch. His desire for her eclipsed his ambition. When she demanded the moon, he reached for the stars. Since he couldn't hand over my share, he took the plunge and resorted to robbing our joint assets and cheating our partnership, giving her everything else he could muster—cash, and yes, even our employees. His love for her and his desire to break free from our partnership not only ruined everything but turned a decades-old partnership into a battlefield.

Now, with Liv's presence looming in every corner of the office, I'm constantly reminded of the aftermath, the ruinous path of a love-struck fool. Because if I give in, if I even entertain the idea of us, I risk being swept into the same storm that claimed Brad. And I can't have that. Not when every dollar in the bank, every contract on the table, represents a piece of me. She's a temptation wrapped in innocence, an enigma that's got my head spinning and my principles teetering on a knife's edge.

I can't afford to fall. Not like Brad. Not for her or anyone.

Caught in a back-and-forth of hypotheticals and impossibilities, I shake my head to clear the fog. It's time to focus on the present—the work, the team—and Liv as one of my Art Directors, rather than thinking about her as a potential date. I accept this challenge with a determined click and put away my phone.

I stand up and stretch out my tense muscles before walking, which leads me unconsciously down the path toward the pit. I seem to find myself there more often these days. As I approach, I see Liv hunched over her work and stop at her desk, clearing my throat. "How's the campaign shaping up? Are you managing with Vicky?" My curiosity is genuine. Vicky has been demanding a lot from everyone since she took over for Mia, and Mia's shoes were big ones to fill. There was a mass exodus when Brad left with his lies, so our resources are limited, but I believe in promoting from within, so Vicky got the job.

Liv looks up at me. "Vicky has definitely made an impression," she says, leaving me unsure if she's impressed or wary.

Glancing at my watch, I realize it's past quitting time. "You should call it a night," I suggest to Liv.

"Just tying up loose ends," she says, keeping one hand on her tablet as she dives back into designing.

I lean against the wall of her cubicle, already plotting my next move. "How about we take a break? I'll order in—my treat."

There's a brief pause, a hint of hesitation. "Takeout sounds nice, but it didn't go well the last time you ordered for me." She points to herself. "I'm picky with food."

"Vegan, I got it." How could I ever forget? "How about a vegan pizza? And although my first attempt at surprising you failed, I think you should give me another chance."

"Sure, as long as you don't surprise me with any ducks," she jokes.

"I will stick with an earth-friendly menu this time," I assure her.

"Sounds good," she agrees before diving back into her work. I quickly place the order, and within thirty minutes, I am back at her desk with a hot and delicious-smelling pizza. "Dinner is served," I announce as I hold up the box filled with savory aromas of oregano and roasted vegetables.

"I'm starving," she admits, shutting down her computer and following me to a table in the corner of the break room.

Remembering our previous experience, I scan the area for anything flammable.

"Prepare yourself for the grand reveal," I announce, my hands hovering over the lid. "I present to you, late-night office dining." I lift the top, unveiling the gourmet vegan masterpiece. "I've ordered vegan pizza, artfully adorned with a medley of wild mushrooms, roasted red peppers, and a drizzle of truffle oil," I declare, as if it's a priceless artifact rather than a pie. "I left off the vegan cheese because I didn't want there to be any doubt."

She bursts into laughter, the kind that's full and true, and when her eyes light up, it's like we've hit the jackpot on a game show. The sight's a reward in itself.

Liv grabs a slice and takes a bite, and the room fills with the moans usually reserved for late-night fun between two consenting adults. "Mmm, this is unreal," she hums, her voice dipping to a frequency that could be sensual, and it does something to me. It speaks to every cell in my body.

I notice a dollop of sauce perched at the corner of her mouth. Without thinking, I reach out and swipe away the rogue red with my thumb. My finger finds my lips, and the taste of the sauce is second to her electrifying glance. Her eyes go wide, the air crackling with a sudden voltage spike. I have to remind myself about the line I can't cross.

But before the current can surge, Vicky bursts in, her entrance like a stampede of buffalos. "Left my phone," she mumbles, but her eyes are laser-focused on Liv, throwing daggers sharper than a pizza cutter. "Why are you still here?" The weight of her stare could crush the average person, but Liv pulls back her shoulders as if she's shoring herself up.

"Because you told me to not leave until I have that damn soybean nailed."

"And do you?"

"Almost."

Vicky snags a slice of pizza, her eyes still locked in a standoff with Liv. "You know what this needs?" she says with the casualness one might reserve for commenting on the weather. "Cheese and pepperoni."

"The whole point was to get something Liv could enjoy." I throw a supportive look Liv's way. "Moreover, it's unfair to ask your employees to work late hours if you're not willing to do the same."

Vicky moves closer, her nails catching the light, each one a tiny masterpiece embellished with jewels. "Had to get these babies touched up." Each word is cocooned in velvet. Her fingers flutter in the air, an invitation for admiration. "You wouldn't appreciate it if I let these go unattended, would you, Seb? It's so important to pay attention to the details."

I offer a half-smile. "Attention to detail is important, but so is employee morale."

"Liv's happy. Aren't you?" Vicky asks.

"As happy as a clam not destined for chowder," Liv says.

Vicky laughs, a sound that flirts with the edge of being genuine. "Glad to hear it." With pizza in hand, Vicky turns, her movement a dance of its own. "I'll leave you to your ... healthy choices," she teases lightly, then looks at me. "Let me know when you're ready to walk on the wild side. There's this great Cuban place a few blocks away. They have the best pork sandwiches."

Thinking of Liv's first date confession, I say, "That's not someplace Liv could easily join us."

"I know." Pausing by the door, Vicky throws a glance back that's all cat-and-mouse. "Catch you tomorrow, boss." And just like that, she's out.

When I glance back at Liv, she's got this smirk, like she's just put two and two together and came up with five. "I think she likes you," she says, nodding toward the door.

"Vicky?" I laugh it off, shrugging. "Wouldn't matter. She's not my type."

Liv leans back, a glint of challenge in her gaze. "Seems like you're on her radar, though."

I shake my head, a firm line drawn. "No, that's not happening. I don't mix business with pleasure. Office romances are off-limits. It's all in the policy." The words are a shield. Yet, every time Liv's around, those rules seem less like boundaries and more like lines drawn in shifting sand, hard to see, and even harder to follow.

Liv leans in closer. "So, what kind of person do you usually go for?" she asks in a lighthearted tone.

Her question sends a ripple of tension through me. She's exactly my type, but I'm not prepared to share my thoughts—not yet, maybe not at all. So, I retreat behind a shield of humor, my go-to safeguard from revealing too much.

"An apocalypse survivalist with a thing for recycling," I say, the corners of my mouth stretching into a grin. It's a dodge, keeping us on the breezy side of chitchat. I'm halfway to dropping the act, spilling the beans, and telling her that I was wrong and perhaps I like a pyro theatrics vegan girl who works for me, but I don't. "Don't stay too late." I stand up from my chair and leave the office because if I stay longer, we might share more than just pizza.

THE FOLLOWING days whizz by with client calls and creative briefs. I steer clear of Liv, not because I want to, but because it's safer that way. I pour myself into prepping for Saturday's challenge, letting the thrill of a possible meet and greet fill me. Part of me wishes I could redo the La Lumiére date, but what good would that do? There are certain lines a man shouldn't cross. I have to focus on what's possible—a butterfly flitting around the tea gardens.

Leaving the office, there's a bounce in my step. I'm ready for the weekend and whatever awaits. Back home, I carefully lay out my clothes, each piece an ally for tomorrow's date.

In the quiet of my room, the night before the challenge, I think about the butterfly avatar, my anonymous match. Will I recognize her? Have we crossed paths already, or exchanged a casual glance at the gas station, or shared a smile at the local coffee shop without knowing it? The app's mystery angle has got me. It's clever, keeping the faces hidden and making me wonder and look around more. It's got me thinking about every chance encounter.

I switch off the lamp, letting the darkness fold around me, and the thought lingers. Perhaps tomorrow, at the Japanese Tea Gardens, amidst the whisper of leaves and the murmur of distant conversations, I'll finally connect a face to the avatar and erase Liv's every time I think about who it could be. And possibly, I'll discover that we've been orbiting each other all this time.

———

I'M BARELY out the door, my mind already on the day ahead, when the universe throws in a fender bender right there in the street. My car's newfound affection for the one in front of it, marked by the groan of crumpled metal, is a jarring start to what should've been a smooth day.

Time has turned on me, every tick of the clock mocking me. Plans for a quick ride to the Tea Gardens are toast, and here I am, swapping insurance info with a guy who looks as thrilled as I am.

With my heart racing and the clock ticking down, I finally break free and arrive at Golden Gate Park. I have a moment of relief when I find a parking spot, but I realize I'll never reach the gardens by eleven on foot. Desperate to make my butterfly mystery date in time, I spot a Segway rental booth. I hastily fill out the paperwork, hand over my credit card information, and hop on. I'm like a modern-day knight ready to conquer San Francisco.

As I ride past pedestrians, I am fully immersed in my realm with the Segway as my noble steed. The Tea Gardens beckon to me, just waiting to reveal their secrets, and this two-wheeled gizmo is my ticket to get there swiftly.

The wind whips through my hair as I zip along the winding paths and vibrant greenery of the park. This is no mere mode of transportation, but an adventure in itself.

This Segway's got a wicked streak, jerking around as if it's trying out for a circus act. Up ahead, the Japanese Tea Gardens unfold like a scene from a tranquil painting, with their meticulously trimmed hedges, winding stone paths, and the arc of the drum bridge reflecting in the calm pond waters. I turn right, but the hyperactive scooter goes left, and suddenly, I'm airborne until I splash down in the koi pond.

Soaked to my ego, I look up, and who's there on the bridge, scoring my landing? Liv, of course. Her laughter's a silver lining.

She holds up both hands, spreading her fingers apart. "I'd give that a ten. You nailed that landing. And look at you, all wet again!"

CHAPTER NINE

LIV

Seb surfaces, soaked to the bone. His hair is plastered to his forehead, and rivulets of pond water stream down his face. He looks like a half-drowned cat forced into an unexpected bath.

I burst into uncontrollable laughter at the sight. It's a full-bodied laugh that rumbles from deep within my chest and may even include a snort or two. Seb glares at me with furrowed brows, making me laugh harder. I make my way to the water's edge. "Admit it—this is pretty hilarious."

He struggles, weighed down by his drenched clothes, so I take pity and extend a hand to help pull him out. His grip is firm as he takes my hand, and together, we haul him onto the grassy bank. It's a surprise to see him, but I'm not surprised. Something inside me had a feeling he'd show up, or I was hoping against all odds.

"Ugh, I'm completely soaked," he grumbles, shaking off excess water like a wet dog. But despite his frustrated tone, I can see the corners of his mouth twitching upwards.

As I take in his soggy state, I can't stop the residual chuckles from escaping. "What happened anyway?"

"The Segway malfunctioned," he says, glancing back at the vehicle sitting on the grass nearby.

"It's possible it didn't care for its driver," I tease.

He narrows his eyes in annoyance. However, there's a slight twitch to his lips that exposes his true emotions. "Clearly not. It threw me off like I was an untrained bull rider."

"Are you trained?" A bubbling sensation fills my chest, a giddy happiness at this unexpected interaction. Something contagious about his damp disgruntlement makes me want to keep bantering and laughing with him.

"It was my first try, and probably my last."

"Come with me. Let's get you dry." I guide Seb toward the teahouse along the winding garden path, his shoes squishing in the damp earth.

As we approach the quaint building, the sweet scent of blooming flowers dances in the air. I greet the staff at the entrance with a wave. "Hey, Tadashi. Hey, Mei."

"Liv! Good to see you," Tadashi says warmly, his dark eyes crinkling at the corners. As his gaze falls upon Seb, they widen in surprise and concern. "Oh dear, what happened here?"

"Just a minor mishap with a Segway," I explain with a smile on my lips.

Tadashi chuckles understandingly. "You aren't the first, and you won't be the last."

Mei clucks her tongue sympathetically as she hurries over to us. "Let's get you dried off."

With swift efficiency, they gather towels and one of the tea house uniforms for Seb to change into. Their kindness and care envelop him like a comforting hug, easing any tension or embarrassment from his accident.

"I'm so sorry about this," I say as Tadashi leads a dripping Seb toward the changing rooms.

"Not to worry, Liv," he assures me. "We'll have your friend sorted in no time."

Seb shoots me a rueful look over his shoulder as he's ushered away.

I take a seat and tug at the hem of my dress. It's a timeless little black number with white piping and gold buttons. As I wait, I question everything. This was supposed to be a casual meet-up, right? A simple tea in the park, not some high-society garden party. Yet here I am feeling like an overdressed cupcake in a bakery full of peanut butter cookies.

My mother's voice, laced with years of unwavering opinions, sounds in my head, "Darling, one can never be too dressed up, or too educated." I roll my eyes skyward as if I could spot her there among the clouds, wagging a finger at me. But then, there's a whisper of a smile on my lips because, despite the slight ridiculousness of it all, I feel ... elegant, poised. After all, I did not hurl myself into a koi pond trying to stop a contraption I didn't know how to ride.

I settle in to wait.

Despite the rough start, there's a sense of comfort in

being here at the tea house. It's like wearing my favorite sweater. I sigh, satisfied, taking in the sweet smells of soil and flowers around me. No matter what else is happening, this place is home. So, when the app directed me here, I was thrilled. And to top it off, they even have vegan almond cookies just for me.

At the teahouse, I'm surrounded by warm wooden walls and the soothing scent of matcha. A server quickly brings over my usual jasmine tea and a plate of vegan cookies. As I take my first sip, Seb appears, looking more comfortable in the tea house uniform.

"Looking sharp," I tease as he sits across from me.

He brushes his hand over the crisp cotton shirt. "I know, right? I make this look good."

As much as I want to remind him that arrogance is not an attractive quality, the words stick in my throat. Because deep down, I know he's right. The uniform, which would have been plain on anyone else, somehow becomes a fashion statement when Seb wears it. He transforms it into an ensemble that could grace any runway.

I hide my grin behind my cup of tea. It's ridiculous, unexpected, but undeniably true—Seb can make anything look good, even a simple tea house uniform.

Tadashi brings tea and cookies for Seb. As we sit and enjoy, our conversation flows effortlessly, and the room's coziness envelops us. "So, are you here for another blind date?" he asks.

It's like the universe is thumbing through a comedy script, throwing us together just after he laid down the law about office romance. Yet, there's no denying the spark, the way my heart trips over itself when he smiles. But I'm keeping my cards close to my chest, locked up tighter than the cookie jar on the highest shelf. I shake my head and take a nonchalant sip, hiding behind the steam rising from my cup. "Just enjoying my usual weekend tranquility. Why are you here?"

"It seemed like a nice day to visit the park. I was heading toward the flower gardens, but the Segway had a mind of its own and drove straight here."

I tuck a strand of hair behind my ear and wonder if this is a random encounter or the app magic at work? Is he truly the stag beetle? And why does the thought make me dizzy with excitement? "That's quite a detour, considering the Conservatory of Flowers is on the other side of the park."

He fidgets with his hands. "Well, I don't want to disturb your tranquility. I can leave if you'd like," he offers, but he stays rooted to the spot. He's not going anywhere, and we both know it.

"No, stay. Tea is always better when shared. So are cookies." I can't deny how nice sharing this place with Seb is. And I wonder if we're both lying to ourselves and each other about what brought us here.

Seb leans back in the booth, looking far more relaxed now than moments before.

"Who knew a Segway could be so temperamental?" He launches into a dramatic retelling of his "watery adventure," as he calls it, complete with wild hand gestures. In this tranquil tea house, bonding over laughter and tea is natural. Unlike when he comes by to check on me at the office and Vicky swoops in like a hawk staking claim to her prey.

I study Seb over my teacup, taking in the glint of humor in those blue eyes. Emotion stirs within me, but I push it down. There will be time later to unravel whatever this is that's transpiring between us. For now, I allow myself the simple joy of having tea with Seb.

My phone suddenly pings, breaking the easy connection between us. I glance down to see a new question in the Love Bug app.

Within the history of these gardens lies a tale of two elements: water, ever-flowing and adapting, and stone, steadfast and enduring. Which element do you resonate with more in love and life?

At that exact moment, Seb pulls out his phone. Our eyes meet across the table, an acknowledgment passing between us. Is he getting a message from the app as well? The possibility sends a little thrill through me, though I keep my expression neutral.

"It's my mother confirming our weekly dinner." I close the app and stuff my phone back into my bag.

"Mine says to pick up my dry cleaning."

He says it with such practiced ease I almost believe him. But the timing's too perfect, the coincidence too neat. My phone, his phone—both chiming, both of us scrambling for excuses that are flimsier than the napkin under my teacup.

I look at him, trying to read the truth in those eyes. Is he really off to pick up dry cleaning, or is it a cover-up for the question the app just asked? My mind whirls with doubt and a touch of intrigue. Is Seb my stag beetle, whose words have circled in my mind, stirring up a tempest of daydreams and what-ifs?

I bite my lip, a laugh bubbling inside. Here we are, two liars weaving tales, too stubborn to admit we've been caught in the same web of attraction. It's a game, a dance we're both playing a part in, and I wonder—who'll make the first move to peel back the layers of pretense?

We finish our tea and cookies, and he says, "Hey, let me give you a ride back."

"No thanks, I've seen how you drive."

"I meant once I return the Segway. My car is in the parking lot, and I can drive you anywhere you want to go."

His offer lingers in the air, suspended between us. Despite the disastrous outcome, there is a part of me that wants to say yes and finally stop running away from the strong connection we shared when we first met. But a more significant part of me is still hesitant and uncertain.

"Oh, that's alright. I have plans to visit my friend Junie for a while," I say as I gather my belongings. "But thank you anyway. I appreciate the offer."

I stand. "This was really nice." I put enough money on the table to cover teas, cookies, and a sizable tip. "I'll see you around!"

Before he can respond, I hurry out of the teahouse,

my heart racing with excitement and confusion. I need Junie's wise counsel before I decide what to do next.

I rush along the garden path, my steps quickening as I distance myself from the teahouse. Is this all coincidence or is Seb my mysterious stag beetle match? Our banter, our chemistry, it all makes sense. But the more rational part of my brain pumps the brakes. Even if he is, it won't work, because he's the boss.

I take a deep breath, trying to sort through the jumble of thoughts and emotions. I need Junie. She'll help me parse through this and make sense of it all. She's been my anchor through the ups and downs, from my first college crush to the heartache of a breakup. I quicken my pace, eager for the clarity only a loyal friend can provide.

Behind me, I imagine Seb watching me disappear down the path, shoes still soggy from cavorting with the koi. But I don't look back. I continue down the walkway, pull my phone from my pocket, and shoot Junie a text.

I need to talk.

She immediately replies.

I'm here.

I breathe deeply, trying to settle my whirling thoughts and emotions. Doubt and uncertainty are my constant companions in heart matters. I hail a cab and head for her place.

She's at the door when I arrive. "You look like you've got a lot on your mind." She walks inside, plops on the sofa, and pats the spot beside her. "Come on, spill."

I sink down on the couch with a sigh, unsure of where to begin. I look around the room. "Where's AJ?"

"Some game with the guys. Who cares? I need the details."

"It's Seb..." I launch into the whole story, starting from the no office dating policy and ending with the teahouse. Junie listens attentively, interjecting with a few questions along the way. I can almost see her mind working as she takes in all the information.

"So, what do you want?" she finally asks softly. "Forget about stag beetles and algorithms for a moment. How do you truly feel?"

I pause, taken aback by the simple question. Inside I'm hopeful, yet afraid. Drawn to him, but also cautious. My emotions are unstable, like ripples in a pond after someone has jumped in.

"I don't know," I admit.

"I remember a girl who once told me to take a leap even when I wasn't sure either."

I sit there, chewing on my lip nervously as Junie takes on the role of therapist. She's not wrong, but diving into the unknown? That goes against everything I am—I'm the type of person who checks the water depth before even dipping a toe.

"Don't overthink it," she advises.

"I'm not overthinking. I just like to be thorough in my decision-making," I defend myself as Junie rolls her eyes dramatically.

"Come on, even a latte order takes you forever!" she teases, poking fun at my tendency to be thorough.

"Well, there are a lot of factors to consider. Do I want almond milk, rice milk, or coconut?" I laugh, trying to ease the tension building up in my nerves. "But hey, it's just a latte. Not exactly a life-changing decision."

"It's a simple choice for me," Junie says confidently.

"Perhaps for you," I respond with a shrug.

She leans in closer, as if sharing some profound secret. "Think about it. What if you take the leap and find out you have wings? Or at least a cute parachute named Seb?"

I picture him now—Seb with his infectious laughter that could melt glaciers. And in an instant, I have a wild urge to jump without looking.

"I want to leap, but what if he's not there to catch me?" I ask, shaking my head.

Junie gives me a knowing look. "But what if he is?"

I let out a sigh. "Fine, but if I crash and burn, I expect free therapy for life."

Junie's expression confirms she believes this risk is worth taking. Love is a leap, but this time, I may finally stick the landing.

"Okay, now that we've settled that," I say, my tummy growling as if on cue, "I'm famished. Harborview's calling our names. I've got a craving for their veggie dim sum."

Junie jumps up and slides into a pair of her Vans, the pink bedazzled ones she saves for special occasions.

"Harborview it is. Let's eat our weight in dumplings before you dive heart-first into Seb's arms."

CHAPTER TEN

SEB

I stay at the teahouse for another hour enjoying the peaceful tranquility. Before I leave, I express my gratitude to Tadashi and assure him I will return his uniform in pristine condition. He briefly regards me before speaking. "Liv is a wonderful girl. She comes from an excellent family and deserves the best."

Is he saying this because he senses my feelings toward her and doubts my intentions or worthiness? His words linger in the air, adding to the already complicated thoughts swirling in my mind. I nod uncertainly, unsure of how to respond.

"She truly is remarkable," I say. "Does she come here often?"

"Almost every weekend."

My heart sinks because that means this meeting could have been purely coincidence. Stepping outside, the crisp air does little to clear my head as Tadashi's words bounce inside my brain. I find my Segway where I left it at the base of the bridge. Rather than taking another daring ride, I walk it back to the rental booth. The agent greets me with a knowing smirk. "So, how did it go?" he asks, eyeing my disheveled appearance and the bag concealing my damp clothes.

I respond with one of my own. "Let's just say if there was an Olympic event for creative dismounts, I would be on the podium," I reply with self-deprecation lacing my words. "Today, I received a perfect ten for landing in a pond. Consider adding a warning label that says, "Objects in life may change direction more sharply than expected.""

We both laugh, reveling in our newfound ability to appreciate the unexpected. "I'll make a note of it." He hands me the paperwork for the return.

I locate my car in the crowded parking lot and slip inside. My hands instinctively take the wheel as I begin my drive home. My mind drifts to Liv and our shared moment of connection. Every interaction and every vulnerable moment we've shared is on replay. I was almost sure she was the butterfly, but that lingering 10% doubt and Tadashi's words gnaw at me. Did I miss something while I was fixated on her? And that I was tuned into her says a lot. When she's around, nothing else matters. It's all so confusing and overwhelming that I have to pull over and text Ryan. He's the only one who can offer any clarity, or at least provide a distraction from the mess Liv has stirred up within me. After all, he's the one who got me into this situation in the first place. Surely, he can help me navigate through it.

Need to talk. Dinner? I type out, struggling to find words to convey the chaos that seeing Liv has unleashed.

Ryan responds quickly.

Sure thing. What about Harborview in an hour?

I'll be there.

I rush home to change out of the borrowed uniform. I fold it neatly and mark my calendar to return it clean and pressed to Tadashi.

Slipping back behind the wheel, I navigate the streets toward Harborview. The name still strikes me as an odd choice for a Chinese restaurant. You'd expect a seafood joint or some dockside bar with that name, not a place serving kung pao chicken and beef with broccoli. But there it stands, with a view of the water that justifies its name and an essence that defies the expected.

As the skyline opens up to reveal the harbor, I'm reminded of how first impressions can be so misleading. My first date with Liv was like Harborview—unexpectedly off-kilter, nothing as it seemed. There was an authenticity in the chaos, a raw, unfiltered series of moments that peeled back the layers of who Liv and I were supposed to be, revealing who we actually were.

We laughed it off afterward, our shared disasters becoming private jokes nobody else would understand. We agreed to reset, to chalk it up to a bad night, but it wasn't all bad. Nobody died, and we walked away with stories to tell. Given today's debacle, we are even in that department.

I park my car at Harborview, cut the engine, and step out into the cool air. Walking inside, I spot Ryan at a table by the window.

"You look like you've had a day," he says, his eyes lighting up with concern and curiosity.

Settling into my chair helps ease the knots in my stomach. "You could say that," I reply, taking a deep breath. "It's Liv. She's driving me crazy."

Ryan leans in, the ever-present humor in his eyes giving way to a more serious sheen. "Talk to me. What's going on?"

I hesitate, the words catching. "It's just—everything today felt like a sign. The app challenge, Liv being there, the pond—"

"Wait. Liv was there?"

"Yes, but she denied going there for a date. I mean, honestly, I don't even know if she's using the app, but it's got to be more than coincidence, right?"

"Exactly," Ryan agrees, his tone turning earnest. "Liv being there is more than it appears. If you believe she's the butterfly the app matched you to, then that means not only did people who know you both think you're a good match, but a scientific algorithm lined you up, too. The universe can't be much clearer. Seems like all signs point to Liv."

"But every time we're together, something outrageous happens. There seems to be a theme of fire and water."

"They say opposites attract."

I let out a long breath, the tension in my shoulders easing. "So, I'm not crazy for thinking there's something there?"

"Not at all," he reassures me. "Look, you've got a double confirmation there. She keeps showing up in your path. There's no way that's an accident. If the universe is speaking, it's time to listen."

The idea resonates, a mixture of relief and anticipation washing over me. "But what about the no-dating-at-work policy?"

Ryan gives a dismissive wave. "Policies are guidelines, not handcuffs. You set the tone. You make the rules."

"I know, but I just made the rule, so I can't change it because it's convenient."

"Why not? You're the boss. You can do whatever you want. Anyway, that rule was to avoid another Brad running off with another Mia and wrecking your business. That's a very unlikely what-if." Ryan leans forward, his eyes locked on mine. "Life's too short for "what-ifs." You've got a seemingly good thing staring you right in the face. Don't let fear or rules born from fear dictate your happiness."

"But I've seen what that does to the environment. My team is counting on me to stay focused. If we don't land this campaign, it affects all of us."

"So, you're going to ignore the signs?"

"I have no choice. Besides, it's all probably a coincidence."

The door to Harborview opens, and a silhouette I recognize immediately is etched against the fading light of the day. I don't have to see her clearly to know it's her. She has this way of altering the room's charge, a soundless announcement of her arrival. My jaw drops open.

"What's wrong?" Ryan asks.

Settling deeper into my seat, my gaze lingers on Liv. She navigates the elegant interior, each step a beat pounding inside my ribcage. "She's here."

"Liv is here?"

I nod. "Can you believe it?"

"And you think this is a coincidence?" Ryan's gaze drifts to where mine is anchored. "Well, I'll be damned," he murmurs. "She's gorgeous. Dude, if you don't move on that, I will."

I level a glare at him that says what I won't—*she's mine.*

CHAPTER ELEVEN

LIV

The atmosphere of Harborview embraces us, the sound of dishes and woks filling the air with comfort. It's a world away from the chilly San Francisco evening we just escaped. My eyes lock on a familiar figure as we scan for an open table.

"Oh my God, Junie, he's here," I whisper, barely able to hear my own words over my heart pounding in my ears.

"Who?" Junie asks, following my gaze across the restaurant.

"Seb," I reply, his name carrying a weight of emotions. "And he's looking right at me."

Junie looks at him and lets out a low whistle. She leans closer to me. "Wow, if George Clooney and Chris Hemsworth had a baby, it would be Seb," she giggles.

I stifle a laugh and shake my head slightly. I don't see the Clooney comparison, but I can see the resemblance to Chris Hemsworth. Those piercing blue eyes? They're definitely something I could get lost in. But as exciting as Seb's presence is, his no-office-romance policy looms over us like an unwanted chaperone. "We have to leave," I say urgently.

"Why? What's wrong?" Junie asks, oblivious to the invisible chains holding me back.

"Because I'm not ready for this," I admit, the truth ringing louder than I intended.

Junie's hand holds onto mine tightly, a lifeline in this sea of people. "Give him a chance, Liv," she insists, pulling me toward Seb.

I let myself be guided by Junie's unwavering conviction until we are standing in front of him, his gaze never leaving mine.

"Good evening, Liv," he greets me, and suddenly, every moment we've shared comes flooding back—the glances, the coincidental encounters at the coffee machine, even our late-night vegan pizza dinner.

I try to say hello back, but the word gets stuck on my lips, held back by the memory of his words. "I never mix business with pleasure." The irony is not lost on me as we stand here in yet another chance social meeting. Rom-coms have fewer twists than this. If they didn't, they wouldn't be believable.

For a moment, I am frozen in place like a statue, unable to move or speak. But then Junie's unyielding spirit breaks through my resistance like sunlight melting frost. She extends her hand confidently. "I'm Junie."

The man next to Seb responds first. "Hi, I'm Ryan." Seb's friend exudes effortless charm. He warmly shakes

Junie's hand, and her smile widens in response. Seb then introduces me to Ryan.

Ryan extends an invitation for us to join their group at their table. I intend to decline politely and pull Junie away, but she speaks up with eagerness. "We would love to!" Her enthusiasm cuts through my hesitation like a sharp knife. "But only if we're getting dim sum."

"By the plateful," Ryan says.

"Then we're in," Junie says.

I give her a look that is equal parts disbelief and frustration, but she just shrugs. "Come on, it'll be fun!"

"Let us take care of that for you," Ryan offers as he and Seb move together to pull out chairs for us. I catch Junie's amused glance as she gracefully sits in the chair Ryan holds out for her.

I turn toward the remaining chair next to Seb. Our eyes meet, and there is a flicker of understanding between us. He pulls the chair out further, signaling me to sit down. There's a surge of awareness as I do. The proximity is almost overwhelming. Our legs brush against each other under the table, creating an electric connection that could light up the San Francisco skyline or steam our dumplings without the kitchen.

As I settle into my seat, the heat from Seb's leg radiates through the fabric of my dress, a subtle yet powerful sign of his presence.

I try to focus on the menu, but it's like reading through a dense fog.

Junie is already chatting away with Ryan, her laughter comforting amidst this unfamiliar setting. I sneak a quick glance at Seb and find him looking at me, his expression a mix of amusement and curiosity. I glance away, and my heart skips a beat.

The dinner begins with a subtle sense of uneasiness, which can be felt in the air lingering around our table. My attempts to take part in the conversation are feeble, with my responses consisting mainly of nods and murmurs instead of actual contributions. Seb's presence beside me, his leg occasionally brushing against mine, sends distracting sensations through my body, causing my thoughts to scatter like leaves on a windy day.

Being ever-observant, Junie picks up on my discomfort. With a not-so-subtle kick under the table, she sends a clear message. "Snap out of it, Liv." I shoot her a sharp look, but it softens as she looks back at me, as if urging me to step out of my comfort zone.

Taking a deep breath, I turn toward the group and force myself to focus on their conversation.

"What do you do for a living, Junie?" Ryan asks.

"I'm the developer for the Love Bug app."

Ryan's eyes widen in surprise. "Really? I knew Liv was the graphic designer, but you're the developer? That app is a masterpiece from top to bottom."

I sit there, slightly stunned. Ryan's impressed by my work on the app, and a small part of me swells with pride. But then it hits me, if he knows about my involvement, that means Seb must have mentioned me to him. The thought sends a strange thrill through me.

Lost in my thoughts, I almost miss Ryan's following words. "You know, I wish the app's art captured my masculinity better," he says. "I'm represented as a firefly, but inside I'm more like a lion." He flexes his arm, and I burst into laughter. It's absurd and comical, but at that moment, it's exactly what I need to let down my walls.

Junie chimes in, saying, "Oh, Ryan, don't let it bother you. My husband's avatar was a ladybug." She proudly shows off her wedding ring. "And look at us now—happily married."

Ryan joins in on the laughter, saying, "I'd rather be a firefly than a st—" But he's interrupted by a sudden movement under the table, and Ryan grunts. There's a brief exchange of glances between the two men in silence.

Ryan recovers smoothly, though his cheeks are tinged with a telltale flush. "I mean, I'd rather be a firefly than a stink beetle," he says, forcing a laugh.

I catch that wordless conversation, my mind piecing together the clues with the thrill of a detective during a pivotal moment in a case. My heart does a somersault. Seb's definitely my match. He has to be. Why else would he kick Ryan? And that st wasn't for stink but for stag. I know it in my heart.

Junie's eyebrows shoot up. "Stink beetle? That's not even an avatar option."

A ripple of chuckles makes its way around the table once more, but my thoughts are elsewhere.

As more puzzle pieces fall into place, the edges remain blurry, but the overall picture is becoming more apparent. One thing's certain—tonight just got a lot more interesting.

The server appears at our table with impeccable

timing, poised to take our order. "Are you ready?" he inquires, pen pausing over his notepad.

Seb turns to me, his eyes asking for me to lead. It's a respectful gesture, one that warms me more than I anticipated.

"I believe we are," I reply, returning Seb's look with a nod. I order my usual from Harborview—vegetable dim sum and plant-based stir fry—and add a request for extra chili on the side. Remembering my match's biggest mistake and response, I add, "I like my food spicy, something that awakens the senses."

Seb's eyes widen as if he understands exactly what I'm doing. I'm calling him out, but he doesn't acknowledge it any further.

"And for the lady," Seb smoothly addresses the server, "please ensure her meal is free of animal products. She prefers cruelty-free options."

There is a moment of quiet as his words sink in, and I am pleasantly surprised. Seb remembered something that matters to me. It may seem small, but it means a lot. It shows thoughtfulness and kindness, and my heart is lighter and warmer. I am grateful for this man who has set boundaries we cannot cross and sad because I want to cross them.

The server nods and notes Seb's order. As he places his order in his familiar rumbling voice, I find comfort in the sound. The server moves on to take Junie and Ryan's orders, giving me a chance to sneak another look at Seb and reassess him.

"Speaking of the app," Junie interjects, turning to me

with that glint in her eye that means she is about to reveal all my secrets to the table, "Liv here is an amazing—"

My foot instinctively kicks out under the table, hitting Junie's shin with a plea for her to stop.

Junie lets out a tiny yelp. "Oops, my bad," she says while rubbing her leg. "Just a leg cramp."

Seb raises an eyebrow, wordlessly questioning what just happened. But Junie ignores it and continues talking to Seb. "Anyway, you're fortunate to have Liv on your team. Not only is she a skilled graphic designer, but she is also the foundation of Love Bug. Our app wouldn't have achieved this level of success without her unwavering dedication and talent. She has a knack for encouraging people to step out of their comfort zones and take risks they wouldn't normally take."

A blush creeps up my neck, making me realize how flustered Junie's words make me. I am about to object and downplay my role when Seb's gaze stops me.

"That doesn't surprise me," he speaks softly and sincerely. "Liv's talent was clear from the moment I saw her. I was captivated. I mean, her work is captivating."

Junie nods knowingly. "We all know what you mean."

"And we agree," Ryan chimes in.

The rest of the dinner unfolds with an ease that surprises me. Conversation flows effortlessly, laughter fills the air, and a comfortable sense of camaraderie settles over the table when our food arrives. We dig into our dishes, the tension fading as we share stories and clink our cutlery.

Seb's proximity creates a pleasant buzz against my

skin—a sensation that was once unsettling but now is grounding and reassuring. He adds his clever wit to the conversation with quiet self-assurance, his laughter a sound I eagerly take in.

As the meal ends, the server discreetly places the check beside Seb's elbow. Without hesitation, Seb reaches for it and insists on paying, brushing off our protests quickly. "It's my pleasure," he reassures us.

The evening wanes, and as we stand to leave, Seb's gaze latches onto me with an intensity that seems to reach past the professional boundaries he's set. "Thank you for joining us. It would be great to do something again," he says, and for a moment, it's like an invitation to something more, something forbidden.

Junie, still buoyant from the night's conviviality, says, "It was almost like a double date, right?" Her teasing tone reveals a hint of truth beneath the surface.

Before I can agree, reality hits me. "Seb is my boss, not a date," I quickly clarify, though a part of me longs to challenge his self-imposed boundaries. "And AJ wouldn't be happy if you started dating Ryan."

"As charming as Ryan may be," Junie replies before turning her gaze directly toward Seb. "The app never lies, and AJ is the only man for me."

"The app says a fruit fly is waiting to meet me," Ryan interjects.

We all laugh together, enjoying each other's company and the potential for something more. Yet we remain within our limits tonight. Lines we won't or can't cross.

"Goodbye," I say, stepping back and becoming aware

of the weight of the unbridgeable gap between Seb and me. Junie follows suit, her earlier boldness softened into a friendly and respectful distance.

Seb's gaze lingers on me for a moment longer before he nods and turns away.

Stepping out into the San Francisco night, the chill of the air is refreshing after the restaurant's warmth. Junie hooks her arm through mine, pulling me close as we walk.

As soon as we're a safe distance away, she leans in, her voice a conspiratorial whisper. "Girl, you better jump on that like a trampoline at a kid's birthday party. That man is a treasure, and tonight's dance of glances didn't lie —it's clear he's into you."

"Jump on that?" I ask. "Please, I'm more likely to jump on a live grenade. It's less risky."

As we flag down a taxi, I take a deep breath and try to reconcile my feelings with logic, knowing that sometimes what seems warm and promising is just an illusion against the cold reality of what actually is.

CHAPTER TWELVE

SEB

The comforting sound of the espresso machine fills the kitchen as I lean against the counter, watching the dark liquid pour into my cup. It's become a daily ritual, grounding me before the busy day begins. As I grab my phone, a notification from the Love Bug app appears on the screen, causing my chest to tighten.

You haven't replied yet. Respond within 24 hours, or your match will flit away.

My match, a butterfly, holds a significant meaning far too delicate for words. The thought of her disappearing weighs heavily on me. It must be Liv. I'm almost sure of it, especially after the spicy comment. The idea of someone else connecting with her, even through an app, makes me uncomfortable. I know I can't have her entirely because of the boundaries I've set for myself, but I also can't bear to lose her to some random matching algorithm.

I take a sip of my scalding hot coffee and let its bitter

taste awaken my senses as I ponder the question I've been avoiding.

Am I water or stone? Which one am I?

In this modern, pristine kitchen with stainless steel appliances and perfectly organized spaces, I am alone and seemingly as unyielding as my granite countertops. But then, thoughts of Liv's contagious laughter and graceful approach to challenges hit me, making me question my nature.

Still savoring the taste of espresso on my tongue, I type out my response—a truth I had not fully admitted until now.

I am drawn to the strength and steadfastness of stone, but I admire the resilience of water. It carves its way around, through, and over any obstacle.

With a final click of the send button, a decision is made. This moment parallels my life—my adherence to self-imposed rules resembling stone, while my growing feelings for Liv are like water finding a path through my defenses.

I finish my coffee, savoring the rich aroma as I place the mug in the sink. Grabbing my keys, I leave the house and lock the door. The weight of my answer lingers with me. It could be that it's not about being completely one or the other—stone or water— but about what we allow to shape us. As I walk away from my house, there's a sense of anticipation creeping up within me. What will Liv say if given this same question? How will she continue to shape me today?

Stepping off the porch, I chuckle at how, just Saturday, I was in such a rush because of Liv and her chaotic impact on my life. That rush ultimately led to a fender bender, which is an analogy for my current predicament. Every moment with Liv is filled with unexpected delights and pandemonium.

But Saturday night at Harborview was different.

I slide into my car, the leather cool against my suit. As I drive, my mind replays the evening. There were no fire alarms or sudden disasters—just laughter, shared glances, and a sense of ease I hadn't felt in a long time. It was an evening that hinted at endless possibilities. If only I allowed myself to indulge in happy possibilities of "what if."

I pull into the company parking lot, that sense of what could be still lingering like a promise. Pushing through the office's glass doors, I try to realign these thoughts with my CEO persona—composed, in control, impenetrable.

I push through the door to the break room, already imagining the bold taste of the second cup of coffee that really kicks off my day. And there she is, Liv, a solitary figure bathed in the radiance of the morning sun filtering through the window. Her head is tilted back, eyes closed, completely immersed in the scent of her coffee.

"Morning, Liv," I say, the words spilling out with an ease I didn't plan on.

Her eyes flutter open, and her lips curl up. "Seb. Didn't expect to see you in here so early."

I fill my cup, the rich aroma blending nicely with her perfume's light, citrusy notes. Leaning against the counter, I adopt her laid-back stance. "Needed my second cup," I reply, holding the steaming mug close. "Can't face the inbox without it."

We lapse into a comfortable silence, broken only by the soft hum of the office coming to life around us. The clatter of keyboards and the distant ring of phones provide a backdrop to this pocket of calm.

I lean in, my elbow brushing hers. "And how's the weather in your world today?" That comes off sounding more like the line of a cheesy morning weatherman, but with Liv, it's like the most important thing I could ask.

She laughs, a sound that fills the break room, brighter than the fluorescent lights above. "Sunny with a chance of disaster," she replies, and I can see the playful spark in her.

For a moment, the lightheartedness in her response lingers, but then, I offer a word of caution, "Don't let Vicky steamroll you. If you need me to step in, let me know."

She stares at me and shakes her head. "I can handle Vicky."

We continue chatting about mundane topics like coffee and weather, but the subtext hangs heavy in the air, an electric charge that neither of us can ignore. As much as I should leave to protect the carefully orchestrated world I've built, she draws me in like a force of nature. Realizing I should probably get back to work, I say, "Guess I better get to it," attempting to nudge myself to leave.

Liv nods, her gaze lingering a moment too long. "See you around, Boss."

As I walk out, the word "boss" echoes in my ears, and reminds me of our boundaries. But our brief encounter plants a seed of doubt against my self-imposed rules.

Settling into the solitude of my office, I find myself momentarily lost in the sprawling cityscape outside my window—a jungle of concrete aspirations. Jen's voice, cutting through the intercom, reels me back. "Seb, you haven't responded to the charity ball invitation. Should I send your RSVP?"

"Yes, Jen, confirm my attendance," I reply. Charity balls are as much about showcasing brands as saving whales, feeding the hungry, or building a new museum wing, and are a mainstay of being an advertising executive. My mental gears shift back to the mound of work awaiting me. I manage to focus for a few hours but find I need a break from the relentless sea of strategy reports that are my world. Stretching out my muscles' stiffness, I take a walk around the office.

My footsteps echo through the corridors, a steady beat that mirrors my climb to this position. But as I approach the design pit, where Liv works diligently under Vicky's watchful eye, my pace slows instinctively. There is an obvious tension between the two, radiating off them in waves that make my jaw clench involuntarily.

I stand at a distance and observe as Vicky leans in too

close, her saccharine voice grating on my nerves as she crosses boundaries with her words. Liv's shoulders tense up, showing she is struggling to maintain her composure. Suddenly, a surge of protectiveness washes over me, unexpected and intense. I want to intervene and step in, but Liv told me she can handle Vicky.

I watch a bit longer, but it becomes evident that Liv isn't handling the situation as she claimed she would. Her polite smile is faltering, and Vicky's behavior is becoming increasingly inappropriate. It's time to trust my instincts. Back in my office, I summon Vicky. It's time to steer the project back on course and address any unprofessional behavior.

Vicky enters with a too-coy expression, apparently unaware of the professional tone I expect. "Seb, what a pleasant surprise. Time with my handsome boss behind closed doors. How can I assist you today?"

I keep it strictly business, quashing the undercurrent of her words. "Vicky, about the project's latest designs," I start, the firmness in my voice non-negotiable. "They're not meeting our target demographic."

She exhales and rolls her eyes. "It's Liv. I can't get her to rise to the occasion." She steps closer. "I should take over the entire project. I can add more depth. Perhaps we could discuss it over dinner?"

I'm grateful for the desk and space between us. "Let's keep this professional. Dinner won't be possible. You know my policy about office relationships. Liv is a talented designer. Maybe she's not seeing your vision." I think about the pitches Liv was given on day one and wonder if they were truly a test. I also saw what she was working on the night we had pizza and that is not what I'd been given. It's possible the problem doesn't lie with Liv at all but with Vicky. Then again, I think about Liv's past work. They were cartoon bugs. And while cute and spot on for an app called Love Bug, they don't require Picasso-level talent. "I need you guys to work together on this. A lot is riding on it."

Vicky's smile slips, her eyes flashing a brief spark of annoyance. "Of course. I'll rework the designs," she says, turning on her heel with a swish of her skirt, leaving me to contemplate the complexities of office dynamics and my increasingly complicated feelings.

My morning passes in a series of meetings, but each time I step out of my office, I cross paths with Liv. In the hallway, we almost collide, our hands brushing as we reach to gather scattered papers. "Sorry," I say, experiencing the charge of our touch.

"It's fine," she responds, her eyes locking with mine. There is so much said in the silence.

Later, in the copy room, I grapple with a jammed printer. Liv walks in, offering help, but I decline, too aware of the confined space and the tension it brings. Liv leaves, but her presence lingers like a whispered promise.

As the afternoon wears on, my frustrations build, and I seek solace at the gym. On my way there, I pass by the nap room and hear muffled sobs coming from inside. I hesitate but ultimately decide to check on whoever is in there. It turns out to be Liv, sitting on a couch with her face buried in her hands. Concern overcomes my hesitation as I step inside and ask if she's okay.

She looks up, startled, with red-rimmed eyes. "Yeah, I'm fine," she stammers. "It's just allergies." But it's clear that something else is bothering her.

"You can talk to me, you know," I tell her. Liv leans in, her tough exterior stripped away, her problems spilling out like a deck of cards scattered on the table. It's an endless list of grievances that starts and ends with Vicky.

"I'm happy to step in."

She shakes her head. "No, I'll take care of it. I'm not really a confrontational kind of person. I'll deal with it in my way."

I have to respect her wishes. "Okay, but if you need me..." I draw lazy loops on her back, a quiet "I got you" without the words. Eyes locked, we're suspended in a standstill. The air around us vibrates. I stare at her lips, pink and full and kissable. I lean forward then back as if on a teeter-totter of indecision. To kiss or not? That thought hammers in my chest.

Then, in a breath, the moment tilts and the choice is made when my hesitation melts away. Our mouths touch in a tender collision. The taste of her lips is like a forbidden fruit, sweet and tantalizing. Time stands still, and I'm lost in that brief connection's intimacy.

And as we pull away, our breaths mingling in the shared space between us, I wonder if we've just crossed a line that will forever alter the course of our lives. "That was risky."

"Too risky," she says. "People will talk if they suspect. We can't do this. I'll lose all credibility."

I nod. "I know." I'm acutely aware of our decision. Keeping our distance is right. Yet, it seems like I'm walking away from something far more important than any rule.

We leave the secluded nap room, our bodies apart, but our emotions still entwined in an intimate embrace. But just as we step into the corridor, we are met with a sharp interruption—Vicky stands there, her eyes fixed on us with a knowing look. "Quite a policy," she remarks mockingly before swiftly walking away. I can't shake off the feeling that she knows exactly what transpired in the nap room between us.

The rest of my day becomes a strategic game of avoidance. I hole up in my office, drowning myself in mundane tasks and numbing my mind with endless reports. The once comforting walls are now like barriers, keeping me from something ... or someone.

Ryan's words echo in my mind, challenging the rules and boundaries I have set for myself. "You're the boss, Seb. You make the rules." But these rules meant to protect me are like shackles holding me back from truly living. And right now, I'm not the only one making the rules. Liv has a set of her own. Is maintaining order really worth sacrificing our happiness?

As the day winds down and the dim light of evening seeps through the windows, I find myself alone. My desk lamp casts long shadows across the room as I contemplate the Love Bug app's earlier question.

I realize Liv represents the water I aspire to be. She adapts, flows, overcomes—everything I've restrained myself from in my pursuit of stability and control.

As the city lights twinkle like stars falling to earth, I wonder if it's time to reassess the rules I've set for myself. Maybe I need to let the water's flow carve a fresh path in the stone of my life.

I grab my things and head to my favorite restaurant, a half block from La Lumiére and coincidently across the street from Pies Before Guys. I wonder why I'd never noticed the bakery before.

I enter the restaurant, enveloped by the cozy, welcoming ambiance that has become a familiar comfort. George, the elderly server who's shared countless moments with me over the years, gestures to my usual spot by the window.

As George carefully pours a rich red wine into my glass, I'm compelled to share my deepest thoughts. "George," I begin, feeling vulnerable, "have you ever had to choose between love and something equally important?"

George pauses. "Ah, Seb, love is always a choice, right? Let me tell you about my Marie."

I take a contemplative sip of my wine as George settles into the seat across from me with a far-off look of nostalgia in his eyes.

"Marie and I met in a small village in France just after the war ended. She was a baker's daughter, and I was a soldier stationed nearby. But our love wasn't just frowned upon. It was forbidden."

The tenderness in George's voice grows as he describes Marie. "She had this fiery spirit, a zest for life that couldn't be contained. Her father had plans for her future that didn't involve a foreign soldier. Every moment we spent together was stolen and hidden away from prying eyes."

Fascinated by the story that transcends time, I lean in closer and ask, "What did you do?"

A smile tugs at the corners of George's mouth, a bittersweet mix of sadness and happiness. "We made the choice to be together every single day. We'd sneak away in the dark of night, meeting in hidden places like back alleys or by the river. Every goodbye held a sense of uncertainty, but we never let fear dictate our love."

He pauses, his eyes reflecting the dancing candle-light. "One day, we were caught. Marie's father was furious and threatened to send her away. But Marie stood up for our love. She declared it openly in front of everyone. It was one of the bravest things I've ever witnessed."

As he speaks, I am drawn into his story, captivated by the idea of a love so strong it could defy societal norms and overcome anger. "What happened then?" I ask, wanting to hear more.

"We left," George says simply. "Left behind her village, her family, everything we knew. Starting fresh with nothing but each other was difficult, Seb. But we faced every challenge and hardship together. And in the end, that bond truly mattered. We built a life, a family, on the foundation of our choice—to love each other against all odds."

I sit in silence, contemplating George's tale of enduring love. His story is not just a distant memory. It reflects my own fears and desires.

With his narrative complete, George stands up. "Love is a choice, Seb. And sometimes, it means standing against the world. But I can tell you this much—I have never regretted that decision for a single moment."

As George's figure disappears into the distance, his words echo in my mind, stirring something profound within me. In their story, I envision a life where love is not just an element of the equation, but the driving force behind it all.

And then, as if by fate, I glimpse out the window and across the street. Liv is entering Pies Before Guys. It's a sign from the universe that I cannot ignore.

I flag down George to pay my bill. The man shuffles towards me with the urgency of a tortoise in a race with the hare. After what seems like an eternity, I enter the cool evening air, the weight of George's narrative still lingering in my thoughts. Love is and should be a deliberate decision.

My heart yearns for something more than rules and boundaries.

CHAPTER THIRTEEN

LIV

The bell chimes as I push open the bakery door, and the sweet scent of buttery croissants, cinnamon-spiced pastries, and rich chocolate muffins envelop me. Pies Before Guys is my paradise of guilty pleasures, but today, with the weight of recent events on my mind, it's like I'm entering uncharted territory. I need something more from it than just cookies and drinks. Being here is like a hug.

The cozy interior welcomes me. Each mismatched table and chair tells its own story, and vintage signs offer a whisper of the past while framed recipes grace the walls like treasured family heirlooms.

Approaching the line at the counter, I take a moment to peruse the glass display case filled with an array of vegan cookies, each one a tempting morsel of sweetness. My thoughts are a whirlwind. My heart tap-dances, still electrified by the brush of lips in the quiet of the nap room.

When it's my turn to order, I say, "Chai soy latte and

a few of those peanut butter chocolate chunk vegan cookies, please."

Eloise nods and prepares my order. With my latte and a plate of cookies in hand, I seek solace at an empty table by the window, basking in the soft light of the setting sun.

Sipping my drink, the memory of that nap-room kiss loops in my head like the last catchy song—impossible to shake and oddly invigorating. It was a moment of unbridled spontaneity, a spark that had ignited between us. And I have to admit, it left me wanting more. It was like a fly-by kiss, a quick and unexpected encounter. There is not enough data to make an educated guess about his skills in that department, that's for sure. But it wasn't just about the mechanics of the kiss. I'm more intrigued by the reason he kissed me. One thing is clear. My feelings for Seb are far from straightforward, and he has feelings for me.

I'm betting that kiss was Seb's way of offering comfort. I had spilled my heart out to him in a vulnerable moment. I had bared my soul, telling him about my struggles and the tension with Vicky. A tidal wave of embarrassment crashes over me, and I contemplate whether a "professional face-palmer" is a viable career path. Could I go through life with my hand hiding my eyes in embarrassment? At the moment I feel like I could.

Vicky's spiteful reaction had only added to my discomfort. When she saw us coming out of the nap room, her expression had been far from pleased. She even commented on Seb's policies, as if she knew we'd kissed.

It's clear that she's not happy about the situation, and I worry about the repercussions. This workplace drama has me more tangled than a pretzel, and I'm not just in the mix—I'm the twist at the center. Does she have a thing for Seb or is that just how she gets by?

Just as I'm lost in my thoughts, and the complicated mess I've found myself in, my phone buzzes with a notification from the Love Bug app. It's the question about water and stone that I need to answer within 24 hours, or the beetle avatar, which I'm convinced is Seb, will scurry away.

I glance at my phone and consider ignoring it, just as I've been trying to push Seb out of my mind. But something stops me. It's the nagging sense that letting the beetle go would be like cutting off the last thread connecting us. This app is a safe place for us where work rules can't follow. I wonder if that's why neither of us have come clean and admitted to using it.

Sighing, I tap on the notification and reread the question.

Within the history of these gardens lies a tale of two elements: water, ever- flowing and adapting, and stone, steadfast and enduring. Which element do you resonate with more in love and life?

It's a thought-provoking question that goes beyond the surface and delves into the depths of love and existence. And even though I'm not sure what Seb's intentions are with this app, I'm drawn to the possibility of a connection beyond the confines of our workplace.

I take a deep breath and type my response, all the while aware that I'm taking a step further into this uncharted territory.

I'm team water, a twist-and-turn pro, always ready to river dance around life's boulders and ride the rapids, expected or not.

I press enter, and almost immediately, a new message pops up. It's from the beetle avatar, and the response reads:

I resonate with stone but admire water's tenacity to shape its path around, through, and over any obstacle.

As I read his words, a comforting sensation spreads through me. It's not just the eloquence of his response but the way it resonates with me. There is a chance that opposites attract. He being stone and me being water. The funny thing is, most would consider stone to be the strength in that relationship, but water, over time, has the power to shape and smooth even the hardest surfaces. It's a beautiful thought that makes my heart flutter with anticipation. Could it be that we're the perfect balance, each complementing the other in ways we're only beginning to understand?

I can't deny the excitement bubbling within me. This app might just be the bridge that connects us, allowing us to explore the depths of our feelings beyond the boundaries of our workplace.

Lost in contemplation over the message, I return to reality when the chair opposite me scrapes the floor.

"Mind if I join you?" Eloise asks warmly as she sets down a plate of vegan cookies and her cup of tea. "You look like you can use reinforcements."

I nod my head, grateful for the company. "Of course, Eloise. Thanks for these," I say, gesturing to the cookies.

She takes a sip of her tea before turning her attention to me. "You seem like you've had another whopper of a day. Care to share?"

I take a deep breath and decide to tell her everything. After all, Eloise has been a comforting presence in my life for years. "It's been a doozy, Eloise. Work is a mess, and I … I kissed my boss."

Eloise raises an eyebrow, and leans in, her interest piqued. "The hottest gossip I've had this week is Mrs. Brown microwaving her purse instead of her lunch. Your lip-lock is the sprinkle on my cupcake. Please, tell me more."

I recount the day's events, from the unexpected encounter with Seb in the break room to our stolen kiss in the nap room.

"I could use a nap room." She looks over her shoulder, where a door leads into a back room. "The place is too small, but I might be able to hang a hammock between the mixer and the freezer." She looks away as if she's mentally calculating the space. "Do you think I'd get away with it?"

I shake my head. "It's probably against some health code."

"They take all the fun out of everything."

Eloise stops teasing and her expression turns serious. "Life is full of surprises, and sometimes, those surprises lead us to places we never expected, like a kiss in a nap room. Is there a chance that he's the one?"

I furrow my brow, still unsure about my feelings for Seb. "But what do I do, Eloise? I'm attracted to him, but it's so complicated."

Eloise chuckles softly. "Love is often messy and complicated. But it's also one of life's most beautiful and exhilarating things, or so I hear. If your heart is drawn to Seb, maybe it's time to follow it and see where it leads."

I sigh, torn between my logical side and my emotions. "It's just so confusing."

Eloise pats my hand gently. "Sometimes you have to embrace it and trust that everything will work out. Life is too short to let opportunities for love slip away."

As I sit there, nibbling on a cookie and taking in Eloise's wise words, a thought forms in my mind. For so long, I've flowed like water, adapting to the circumstances around me and going where others saw fit. But that won't work with Seb. I may need to adopt a more rock-like persona, unyielding and steadfast in pursuing what I want.

It's a departure from my usual easy-going attitude, but Eloise's offbeat advice is like a compass pointing to "X marks the heart"—and sailing into love has to be the grandest adventure there is.

I gaze toward her and ask, "Have you ever been in love?"

Eloise's eyes sparkle with the secret knowledge of a cat who's found the cream. She leans in conspiratorially. "Oh, Liv, let me tell you, I didn't just fall for a magician—I plummeted like a clumsy acrobat without a safety net. He used to pull rabbits out of hats and make doves disappear into thin air. It turns out that was his superpower. And six months into our relationship, he was gone—poof—and I never heard from him again."

She pauses, her tone shifting from whimsy to sincerity, but with a touch of humor. "But you see, Liv, I learned my lesson. I vowed never to date anyone with supernatural abilities again. From now on, I'm sticking with mere mortals! But I sure did love his wand." Eloise chuckles, as if finding humor even in the most peculiar of heartbreaks. "In the end, it was worth it because for a moment I felt loved."

Her story hits a nerve. Would it be worse to never be in love or to love and have someone break my heart? It's a question that lingers as I contemplate my next move.

"You know, there are some perks to being single. No one to hog the blankets or steal your fries."

A laugh tickles inside me. "That's true. And I can binge-watch my favorite shows with no one judging my choices."

She nods enthusiastically. "Exactly! Plus, you can eat fruit sorbet straight from the tub without sharing."

I see the silver lining in her perspective. "You make being single sound pretty appealing."

She winks at me. "The most important thing to

remember is to love yourself more than anyone could love you. If you can do that, then you're never without love."

The bell above the bakery door sounds, announcing a new customer. I turn my head, expecting to see an unfamiliar face, but my pulse stutters when I lock eyes with Seb—as if our gazes are guided by some mutually built-in GPS. Time seems to slow down for a moment, and the world fades away, leaving only Seb and me in this unexpected encounter.

Catching me off guard, my emotions are a cocktail of surprise, uncertainty, and a flicker of something more profound. It's as if fate has orchestrated another meeting, bringing us together once again.

The bakery is filled with a tense atmosphere, words unspoken and issues unresolved. He approaches me. "Liv, we need to talk," he says, breaking the silence.

Eloise looks up and greets him with a smile. "You must be Seb." She offers him her seat. "I'll leave you two alone."

My heart races as I meet his gaze, not knowing what he will say or do next. The anticipation hangs in the air, like the scent of freshly baked cinnamon rolls. But I don't have to wait long because he leans down and kisses me with such intensity and longing that it's like he's been waiting for this moment his whole life. It's a kiss that tastes like warm apple pie on a crisp autumn day, and I lose myself in its sweetness, savoring every second, transported to a paradise unknown.

CHAPTER FOURTEEN

SEB

As our lips part, a sizzle lingers, a vivid memory of the step we've just taken. I'm standing here, heart hammering like a drum solo in my chest, caught in the aftershock. This kiss, longer and deeper than the fleeting one we shared earlier, seems like a line crossed, a rule rewritten.

The silence stretches between us, thick and weighted. I am aware of the questions hanging in the air, the uncertainty and fear. But now, in the aftermath of our first real kiss, I'm not afraid of what may come from this. Damn the consequences.

I reach out and take her hand, our fingers lacing naturally as I slide into the seat next to her. Her palm is smaller than mine, but it fits perfectly, like a missing puzzle piece finally found. And in this moment, I know I'm exactly where I'm meant to be.

"Okay, that was..." I scramble for the right words, but my go-to polished pitches have deserted me. "Not in the storyboards," I manage, a lopsided grin creeping in.

Her laughter fills the bakery, a melody that seems to reorder the world a little. "Certainly not in my ad copy," she says, her eyes dancing with humor and a hint of something deeper. "And as much as I'd like to deny it, I like where you're going with it."

My mind races back to earlier that day, to the brief, impulsive kiss we shared. It was a moment of madness, a lapse in my usual iron-clad self-control. And now, here we are, diving headfirst into the foolishness.

"I told myself this couldn't happen again." I look away, the reflection in the bakery window not mine—the man there is too full of longing, too reckless with his wants. "But then there you were, and the rules ... they didn't just evaporate. They became irrelevant." I wouldn't tell her about George and the story of a man who had found the love of his life. That might scare her off. Besides, it's too long and convoluted a story to share, so I blame it on my lack of self-control.

"Yes, it all feels silly to deny ourselves." Her gaze holds mine, steady and unwavering. "Seb, we're not robots. We can't just program ourselves to feel or not feel something."

I chuckle. "You're right. My "do not kiss" subroutine apparently has a bug. So," I say, taking a deep breath, "where does this bug in the system leave us?"

She leans forward slightly, her expression earnest. "I think it leaves us at a crossroads. One where we need to decide whether to follow our rules or ... rewrite them."

Rewrite them. The words hang in the air. It's a challenge, a possibility, a replay of what Ryan has recommended several times.

"There's no going back, is there?" I ask, my voice barely above a whisper. Even our whispers are treading on new ground.

Her expression betrays a hint of sadness or fear as she asks, "Do you want to go back?"

I quickly respond, "No, I don't," shaking my head.

Strands of her hair catch the light, transforming them into black threads. She looks at me and says, "Then let's keep moving forward."

My mind is still processing but my feet have already chosen a path before I finally nod in agreement. "We broke a major rule," I point out.

A faint grin tugs at her lips, but there is a sense of gravity in her tone. "Yes, we did," she says. "And it will change things."

I release a held breath and try to see the positive side. "Change can be a good thing, though, right?" I ask, hoping to convince myself as well.

Her laughter blends into the warm ambiance of the bakery as she responds, "It depends on the change, but yes, it can be freeing."

A mix of intense emotions swirls inside me, creating an exhilarating sense of freedom. I lean in toward her, driven by a force that is both familiar and new simultaneously. "So, are we free now? Free to explore whatever this is between us?"

She looks at me with affection. "Yes, I believe we are," she says. "The thing holding us back is your rule and my determination to succeed. Are we willing to change?"

Making this decision together is like stepping into unfamiliar territory, but it's a responsibility and thrill I never could have expected. As I gaze into her eyes, I realize some rules are worth breaking for the right person. "My best friend has reminded me countless times about being the boss and making the rules, as well as breaking them for the right reasons."

Liv raises an eyebrow, her curiosity piqued. "I'm curious about one rule in particular—why no dating in the office? It seems prudent, but why that rule? After all, it's where most people spend the bulk of their lives, and they're likely to meet someone there. I get the boss-employee thing, but what about employee dating? Is there a story behind that rule?"

For a moment, I look away to stare out the window. I share almost everything with her—including the story of Brad and Mia and how their affair nearly destroyed our company and led to Brad leaving, taking Mia and half our team with him to start a rival business. But there's one part I keep to myself—how losing the Soy Joy account could spell disaster for us. I don't want to burden her with that information or pressure her, especially since she's working so hard on the designs for that project. Pressure and worry about losing your job does not make you more creative.

"Change isn't always a negative thing. Perhaps his departure was an opportunity for you to grow," she says.

I take in the view before me, allowing myself to

gather my thoughts. Our reflections are also visible in the window, two figures captured in intense contemplation. "I guess I'll have to consider that," I reply, still trying to process everything that has happened. "But it caused some turmoil, and implementing a no-dating policy was my way of protecting those left behind. It was my promise to not let anyone come between me and the work. Our people and our clients count on all of us. It's up to me to make sure we can deliver. I also implemented a no-poaching employees or stealing clients clause in employment agreements. That should have been obvious, but it didn't occur to me that my business partner and most trusted friend would try to steal the company we built together from me."

"That's awful. I understand, truly," she says with a nod.

I turn back to her, determined to be honest. "But when we kissed," I begin, speaking with newfound conviction, "it felt like something that was meant to happen. It's as if that first night at La Lumiére, if we had kissed then, we wouldn't be here now, struggling to make sense of the boundaries we just crossed. You're talented and hard-working. You deserve to be recognized on your own merits, not whispered about behind your back, or resented by your direct manager because I've always rebuffed her self-serving and frankly very inappropriate advances."

She tilts her head before meeting my gaze again. "When I saw you that night, I knew I'd kiss you."

"Is that right? I guess we've been orbiting this moment since then," I admit, surprised by my honesty.

She laughs quietly. "That date was a mess," she reminds me, but there is no bitterness in her words, only fondness for shared memories.

"It was," I agree. "However, it could have been necessary. So, we could get here, to this unexpected place of appreciation." I look around. "We haven't set anything ablaze since that first day." That's not entirely true I think to myself. My heart's on fire and the rest of my body is beginning to smolder.

"Don't jinx us," she says, but a twinkle in her eye tells me she's not unhappy with the turn of events.

I lean in, my voice dropping to a murmur meant for her ears only. "I've been thinking about this. About you. About us."

"And?" Her single word is an invitation to continue, to bear the thoughts I've kept hidden.

"And I'm tired of thinking," I admit with a half-hearted chuckle. "I want to see where this goes. I've wanted to see that since I felt like a jerk watching you walk away instead of going with you to this bakery. I don't know what I was afraid of."

"Real Soy Joy?" she laughs. "Okay." She bites her lip. "What happens at work? There's a lot at stake for both of us. It's important to me to earn—"

"Your place. I know, so how about at work we remain professional? We do our jobs, and we don't let this," I pause, allowing the whole meaning of *us* to sink in, "change how we operate there. Do you think we can do that?"

She nods. "We're adults. We can handle it," she says firmly.

We shake on it—a deal made in the quiet corner of a bakery that smells of sugar and cinnamon. It's a pact, a division of our lives into compartments that we're both determined to keep separate.

"Can I offer you a ride home?" I ask, the words both ordinary and momentous as they hang in the air between us.

There is a hint of amusement on her lips. "That would be nice," she says, and a light in her eyes outshines the bakery's glow.

Before we leave, Liv says goodbye to the bakery owner Eloise who tells her something about having to share the remote.

"Something I should know?"

Liv looks up at me. "Just girl talk."

The walk to my car combines comfortable silence and stolen glances. I open the passenger door for her, and she slides in, the simple act charged with a new intimacy.

She gives me her address, and the drive is quiet. The city lights blur past, creating a mosaic of motion and color.

When we arrive, I walk her to her door. The air between us is thick with unsaid words and uncharted possibilities. I lean in, and our kiss is a soft echo of the earlier one.

She lingers in the doorway, her hand on the frame.

"Do you want to come up?" she asks with a hint of invitation in her voice.

I pause. Every part of me is screaming yes. But the prospect of our slow exploration whispers caution. "I think it's best if we leave something for tomorrow," I say.

"Tomorrow, then," she states confidently.

"Yes, tomorrow," I confirm with one last glance at her before walking away, still feeling the gentle touch of her lips on mine.

As I return to my car, my phone buzzes with a notification from the Love Bug app. It's the answer to the stone and water question. The timing is almost too perfect—as if the universe is playing along with our unpredictable dance.

I open the message and read the words that light up my screen. Another piece of the butterfly shared. Another step into this adventure we're embarking on together. The night engulfs me as I drive off, and I wonder how I'll survive this willing dive into love's abyss. I immediately decide to experience one moment, kiss, and decision at a time with her.

CHAPTER FIFTEEN

LIV

My heels keep up their relentless beat on the shiny floor. Slipping into my little corner of the corporate maze, I'm greeted by the familiar cocktail of ink and yet unfulfilled dreams.

My computer flickers on, a beacon in the quiet office. But before I can lose myself in emails, Vicky appears like an ad pop-up that I can't block.

"You're going to want to double-shot your espresso today," she says, dumping a stack of folders on my already cluttered desk. They land with a thud that spells "emergency" in big, bold letters. Vicky leans closer. "The soybean campaign isn't hitting the right notes. It's as dry as the cookies pushing. I want cute, I want adorable. Can't you do that thing you did with Love Bug?"

I glance at the drafts, then back to Vicky. "Love Bug magic was special because it spoke to the heart," I tell her, hoping she'll get it. "That kind of charm doesn't just transfer to any product."

Vicky's tapping her nails, a Morse code for "I don't want to hear it."

"Liv, spare me the spiel. I need results. Since you're the vegan whisperer, make it resonate. You know, like those bugs reached out to the loveless."

I take a deep breath, trying to ground myself. "Good campaigns need to resonate with what the audience wants, Vicky. Soybeans and dating apps are different beasts. We've got to dig deep, find what makes our beans the main event."

She hits me with a gaze that could freeze coffee. "Use that energy. We're on a deadline tighter than last year's budget," she says, all business and bluster.

I sigh when she's finally gone, her sharp heels echoing down the hall. Staring down the paper mountain on my desk, I try to find a little humor in the chaos. "You mean deadlines tighter than my jeans after Thanksgiving," I whisper to no one, rolling my shoulders back. Time to be the warrior they pay me to be, one pencil stroke at a time.

Not over ten minutes pass before Seb enters the pit and signals for Vicky and me to follow him. Vicky strides ahead, with a self-assuredness I don't feel. I follow, my heart not in the folders and figures but in the lingering fear of inadequacy.

In Seb's office, the air is thick with expectation. He's perched behind his desk like a judge in the final round of some high-stakes talent show.

Vicky wastes no time, firing up her laptop with a flourish. A cartoonish soybean character winks back at us on the screen, grinning like it's in on some joke I can't hear.

As Vicky pitches with the zeal of a street-corner prophet, I stand there, feeling like a fraud. This isn't me. This isn't my work. It's a caricature of a campaign, born from a brief that gave me no room to question or bend. I watch Seb's face. The growing cloud of disappointment in his eyes reflects my own inner turmoil.

When Seb finally speaks, his words are a polite version of a facepalm. "This isn't it," he says simply, and each syllable is like a personal indictment.

I came to Innovative Advertising to make a splash, to be a drop that ripples out, changing the water around it. But this? This campaign might as well be a leak in the hull, sinking all my dreams of making a difference.

I want to tell him I know it's wrong, that I had no choice but to follow Vicky's path. But I don't. Instead, I stand there, the weight of failure settling around my shoulders like a leaden shawl.

Seb's eyes meet mine, a flash of something like understanding passing through them. "We need to go back to the drawing board," he says, and it's a lifeline thrown into the water. "Both of you. Separate ideas. You'll pitch to the group. The winner gets the campaign."

I nod, a mix of relief and fresh anxiety churning within. In my first project at the ad agency, I have to take on the Creative Director to prove my worth. This is my chance, my do-over. I won't just go with the flow this time. I'll be the current, strong, and sure, carving a new path through the rock. This is personal. This campaign will be my mark, my legacy. Not a cartoon bean, but a message that resonates, that has the potential to transform minds and possibly even a small part of the world.

I return to the pit, where it's a symphony of clicks and murmurs, but at my desk, it's just the tap-tap-tap of keys as I pour every ounce of creativity into the new Soy Joy pitch. The screen beckons, a blank canvas waiting for my pen, ideas, and soul. This isn't just a job. It's the proving ground for every dream I've dared to have since stepping through Innovative Advertising's doors.

Hours slip by in a blur of brainstorming and mock-ups until my stomach growls, telling me that even dreamers need to eat. I push back from my desk, my mind feeling like a junkyard of taglines and visuals, and head to the break room.

Reaching for the last coffee pod, the quiet is shattered by the door swinging open. Seb stands there. We lock eyes, and a spark ignites when our hands touch, reaching for a sugar packet.

Vicky chooses that moment to walk in, her sharp eyes missing nothing. I sense the question taking shape before she even opens her mouth. I retract my hand as if Seb's touch is scalding, but the heat lingers as a warm sensual current rushes through every part of me.

He's quick to retreat, a master of self-control, leaving me with the sugar packet and a heart racing like I've had a triple shot already.

Before I can breathe, Vicky's voice cuts through the quiet. "Liv, got a sec?" Her words no sooner land and Vicky is at my elbow, eyes sharpening with curiosity that's too keen for comfort. She leans in, and I brace for impact. "Is there something going on with you and Seb?" Her question is a dart, and it hits close to home.

Despite the traitorous thump-thump of my heart, I muster a calmness in my voice that feels as thin as tracing paper. "No, Vicky, nothing like that," I lie, the words sticking in my throat. I hate the deceit, the way it coils in my stomach uncomfortably.

She studies me a second longer, a human polygraph, then seems to accept my answer. But as she walks away, I realize I'm not just crafting campaigns but turning into someone I don't recognize—a liar.

Later, Seb's presence near my desk is like a sudden change in air pressure, and I'm hyperaware of him. Every sense dialed up to ten. When our eyes meet, I see the flicker of last night's laughter in his gaze, how he looked under the soft bakery lights, and how his hand felt in mine. My mind is still smelling cinnamon and sugar and tasting his lips.

As he walks away, it's like an invisible cord, spun from those hidden glances, tugging at me. My skin remembers his kiss, a haunting sensation both sweet and agonizing.

The clock's hands crawl, and with each tick, the restlessness builds, accumulating unspent energy and stifled emotions. I can't sit still or focus—every cell in my body is rebelling, buzzing with the awareness of Seb's nearness. Finally, I snap my laptop shut. I need to move, run, and do something with this turmoil that's got me twisted up inside.

I change quickly into my gym clothes, the fabric like a new skin that doesn't know Seb's touch. The gym is my escape, a treadmill, where I can pound out one forbidden thought about the boss at a time to the beat of my "Running from Reality" playlist.

I'm jogging on the spot, the hum of the treadmill beneath my sneakers almost hypnotic. Seb walks in and hits the free weights, flexing more than just his job title. There's something about a man in motion that makes my heartbeat skip to a new rhythm.

"Focus," I mutter, thumbing the speed up a notch. Who needs willpower when you've got horsepower underfoot?

A sly peek over at Seb and—oops! That's one misstep too many. The belt skids beneath me like a banana peel in a cartoon, and I'm a slapstick heroine, arms pinwheeling. It's a faceplant waiting to happen, and the floor rises to meet me with an unceremonious smack.

I'm a sprawl of limbs and bruised dignity, the treadmill chugging on, indifferent to my absence. I shoot up faster than a Pop Tart from a toaster, declaring to a gym that couldn't care less, "I'm totally fine!"

Seb's oblivious, cocooned in his bubble of biceps and barbells. I brush off the imaginary dust. Nothing to see here, folks, just a girl tripping over flat surfaces and her own two feet.

With my heart still doing the samba, I hightail it out of there, ready to bury myself in work and the comforting call of my computer screen. The Soy Joy campaign won't design itself, and at least Photoshop can't make me fall on my face. Right?

I sit back. The chair creaks softly, and I let my thoughts drift to Seb. There's a sweetness in remembering his face, the sound of his voice when he's not Mr. Boss Man but just Seb, talking to me, laughing with me. But it's like tasting chocolate and craving more. How do I navigate a love that's a whisper, a shadow, a thing of stolen glances and half-breaths? How do I hold it close, keep it safe, when every instinct screams to shout it from the rooftops? Isn't love supposed to be shared and celebrated?

The screen goes dark, and there's just me, reflected in the blank monitor—a woman caught in the middle of a secret love that's as intense as it is hidden. I pack up. The thing with Seb is real, but so is the sting of having to keep us secret. Is this the love I was looking for? Sneaking around, whispering, always looking over my shoulder— waiting for Vicky to bitch-slap me with words and eye daggers for taking the man she thought could take her to the top? Secret lovers wasn't the plan, but it was the rule we agreed to.

CHAPTER SIXTEEN

SEB

As the office empties, I'm left alone at my desk, surrounded by piles of work that need my attention. But my mind is consumed by thoughts of Liv.

The connection between us is like an invisible thread, drawing me closer to her every day. How she looks at me, the moments we've shared, and our furtive touches play in a loop in my head.

But as I stare at the computer screen, doubt creeps in. Is this rule-breaking love worth the risk? It's exhilarating yet terrifying, and the constant cover-up is becoming too much to bear. I'm caught in my own trap, and now I've put the woman of my dreams there too. This balancing act of chief executive by day and man of her dreams after hours and in shadows is going to suffocate our seedlings of true love before they see the light of day. Is my rule that important, or is it just another protective layer to guard myself?

I gather my things and leave the office, craving fresh air to clear my mind.

My phone buzzes in my pocket, and I see a notification from the Love Bug app. It's asking me a question.

Fancy dinner and a theater date, or stream a movie and takeout?

It's as though the app can read my thoughts. We barely have time to spend together at work, so after work is our time. And while the app isn't arranging our next date, responding with a question could solve two issues. It would confirm that Liv is my perfect match and bring us together for dinner and a movie night.

I quickly type out a message.

How about we have dinner tonight at my place, around 7 PM? I'll order some delicious vegan Thai food, and we can watch a romantic comedy. What do you think? Are you in?

I include my address and hit send, feeling both nervous and excited. If it is indeed Liv, which deep down I know it will be, she'll see that I'm making an effort for her because, on our first date, I made it clear that I'd rather gouge my eyes out than watch one of those movies, but I'd watch a marathon of terrible 70s commercials just to be with her.

With the message sent, I speed home in my car, mentally creating different scenarios for our evening together. Should I have bought flowers? Do I need to make dessert? Is my house tidy enough?

I arrive home and diligently dive into preparations, channeling my inner Martha Stewart. The vegan Thai food is ordered, and I even add a few extra dishes just in case. As for the rom-com selection, I've carefully chosen streaming options to elicit that happily ever after she loves about them.

My usually quiet, simple home has become a war zone of nerves and anticipation. I meticulously arrange the living room, aiming for a balance between cozy and romantic. Candles? Check. Soft music playlist? Check. An excessive number of throw pillows? Check.

As I repeatedly look at the clock, I laugh at how absurd it all is. Here I am, a grown man turning my house into a love retreat. No one would believe it.

I sit on the couch, constantly glancing at the dating app for a response, but nothing yet. All this planning could be for nothing or everything, I remind myself. I know I've broken all the app rules by sharing personal information like my phone number and address, but I couldn't resist. Somehow, our relationship seems beyond all those rules. And yet, I don't even have her number. I'll have to change that tonight, but I'm at the mercy of this app for now.

In the middle of my excitement, a fearful thought creeps in—what if someone else shows up at my door tonight? What if it's a longshoreman named Bertha, or a toothless grandma named Gerty? I can only hope it's Liv.

Then, my gaze drifts to the wall—a gallery of my proudest moments. Each fish trophy is more than a testament to a successful catch. They are echoes of laughter and lessons from the man who taught me patience and the thrill of the chase. Dad. I can almost hear his hearty chuckle resonating through the room and the soft thud of his reassuring pat on my back. Then it dawns on me, I've just rolled out the red carpet for a woman who's likely got "Fish Are Friends, Not Food" tattooed somewhere. And here I am, the curator of the "Gone Fishin'" exhibit.

Those trophies stare me down, their shiny peepers practically asking, "Buddy, how are you gonna swim your way out of this one?"

"Sorry, Dad," I whisper to the empty room, my hand hovering over a large bass we landed together on a trip that now feels like a lifetime ago. It's hard to believe he's been gone five years. "These guys need to take a time-out tonight. You understand, don't you? For Mom, you once hid your bowling trophies. You said it was to make room for her ceramics, but we both knew you just wanted to make her smile."

I carefully remove the trophies one by one, each a weighty symbol of the bond we shared. "Remember when you let that big pike go because Mom said it looked sad? I think that's when I learned the biggest catch isn't always the one you keep." The memories flow like a river's current, strong, and unbidden, and for a moment, I can almost feel the sun on my face, the boat gently rocking beneath us, and Dad's voice telling me, "Just one more cast, son."

With mixed emotions, I tuck the trophies into the closet. "For tonight, the greatest catch would be Liv's heart. I know you'd do the same." The words hang in the air, a testament to the man who shaped me, the love he showed, and a first bold step toward the lengths I'm willing to go for love.

I give the house one more look before I head to the shower, determined to be squeaky clean for our evening together.

As the water cascades down, I soap up, and my mind churns with a wardrobe dilemma. There's a laid-back option with a comfy T-shirt and jeans that seems to whisper, "I'm all about the cozy vibes," but the memory of past wardrobe missteps looms over me like a fashion police arrest warrant. There was the infamous "Casual Friday" incident of '09, where my under-standing of "casual" included shorts that would have been more at home on a beach in Bermuda than in an office setting. Janice from accounting still hasn't let me live down the sight of my pasty legs during the quarterly meeting.

Or that time in college when dress to impress got lost in translation, and I showed up to a seminar in a full tuxedo while everyone else sported smart casual. The professor had a field day with that, dubbing me "Bond, James Bond" for the rest of the semester. Even now, the thought sends a blush to my cheeks that has nothing to do with the hot water.

So yes, a T-shirt and jeans might be too casual, but they're a far cry from the Bermuda shorts or Bond misstep. Still, I can't risk underdressing again. I switch off the shower, grab a towel, and decide to aim for a middle ground—a happy medium where comfort meets class without the risk of becoming an accidental office meme again.

The Love Bug app pings and I eagerly check the notification. But the response is just one word.

Yes.

I can't decipher from a single word if it's Liv, so all I can do is wait.

As I approach the dining room to set the table, I notice the clock on the wall. It's nearing seven, the time I suggested for our dinner. The anticipation and nervousness swirl in my chest, like a troupe of Rockettes performing a dance behind my ribcage and each high kick slamming into my heart.

Suddenly, there's a knock at the door, and I freeze. Is it Liv? Could she have arrived early?

I take a deep breath and open the door, my eyes filled with hope. But as I look outside, a wave of disappointment crashes over me when I see a six-foot bearded guy holding up two big bags. "Phuket Thai delivery." He thrusts the bags forward.

I force a polite thank you through my disappointment and hand him a tip as he forks over the food. I close the door behind me, attempting to shake off the sense of disappointment. It's not Liv, but at least now everything is ready for our evening together. And if she doesn't show up, this will still be the best date I've ever planned for myself.

I carry the bags into the dining room, inhaling the delicious smell of the food. Giving up meat for tofu and vegetables shows how much I care about this girl. But then again, I kissed her, and she's worth it.

I carefully set the table with plates, utensils, and napkins. With everything perfectly in place, my anticipation grows once again.

The app dings and a warning about breaking the rules flashes across my screen. It says I'm banned from the app for two weeks, and if my match is still there, then it's meant to be. All I can do is hope that she shows up tonight.

I watch the clock tick away slowly. It reaches seven o'clock, then five minutes after, then ten after. Twenty minutes later, I wonder if she's chickened out because I broke the rules.

I'm on the verge of giving up hope when there's a knock on the door.

CHAPTER SEVENTEEN

LIV

I stand at what I hope is Seb's door, my heart pounding in a rhythm of anxious anticipation when the app informs me that we've broken the rules and we're banned from interacting for two weeks. Is this a sign of something bad? Half ready to bolt, I clutch my bag like a lifeline, images of a hasty retreat swirling in my mind. But when the door swings open, revealing Seb's familiar, handsome face, a wave of profound relief washes over me, soothing my frazzled nerves.

"Oh, thank God!" I exclaim, the words tumbling out in a burst of unrestrained joy. "I even thought about stopping by Junie's first, just to borrow a pair of her old sneakers. You know, in case I needed to make a quick getaway, but there was so much traffic, and I didn't want to be later than I already was." I laugh, an airy sound that masks my underlying nervousness. "But deep down, in the quiet place where truth whispers, I knew it had to be you."

Seb's grin blooms like a flower in spring, happy and inviting. The joy in his eyes mirrors my own, reflecting a shared connection. "I'm so glad you're here," he replies, his voice a caress that makes me want to melt into the doorway. He steps aside, an invitation into his world. "I assume you got the message. We're in time out."

I nod as I enter. My eyes dance with curiosity and awe. The living room unfolds before me like a scene from a dream, bathed in the soft, golden hues of strategically placed lamps and the flickering dance of candlelight. Large windows frame the evening sky, now a canvas of deep blues and purples, adding an unexpected touch of laidback charm to the room. The décor strikes a delicate balance between modern chic and homey comfort, each piece of furniture an invitation to unwind.

My gaze wanders, drinking in the vibrant artwork adorning the walls. There's a story waiting to be told by every framed masterpiece, even from the blank wall that shows outlines of art that once hung there. Sculptures maybe? The faint outlines seem uneven. I can't make them out. Bookshelves, brimming with diverse titles, speak of a mind that craves knowledge and adventure. A plush area rug underfoot creates a warm contrast with the polished hardwood, proving that thought was put into every detail of this space.

It's a world away from my compact studio apartment, where practicality is king, and every square foot is a masterclass in space-saving harmony.

I notice a ship in a bottle, marooned on the mantel.

Its sails are set, full, and ready for a voyage on the high shelf seas.

"Love the ship," I say, a grin spreading across my face. It's a tiny, majestic thing, destined to sail the perilous gap between the books and the potted plant, captained by the bravest dust mote to ever hold a miniature wheel. "I bet it's plotting a mutiny for more shelf space," I say, imagining its tiny crew restless for a stretch in the open air. "Still tinkering with it?"

He nods his head, a wistful note in his eyes. "Yes, unfortunately, I got caught up in the hectic pace of daily life and haven't had time to finish it." He leads me deeper into the heart of his home, his movements a fluid dance of familiarity in this personal haven.

He pours us a glass of wine, the rich, ruby liquid, a toast to the evening ahead. We settle onto the couch, now an island amidst a sea of throw pillows, each one an embrace of comfort and style.

"So," he begins, a teasing glint in his eyes, "you almost went for the escape sneakers, huh?"

"What would you have done if it wasn't me?" I ask, a teasing challenge in my tone.

"I hadn't gotten that far in my thoughts because I knew in my gut that it was you. In my heart, it couldn't have been anyone else." His voice is a soft, confident timbre that makes my heart flutter.

"But what if it wasn't me?"

"I just knew it would be you." Seb leans back, his expression thoughtful, sculpted by the flickering candlelight. "And if it wasn't you at the door, I might have had to resort to dramatic tactics. I would have had to say they were at the wrong house, or I didn't speak the language—something out of a bad comedy skit."

But as we banter, a nagging thought creeps into my mind. "Would you have still invited her in?"

His expression fades into one of sincerity, his gaze meeting mine with unguarded honesty. "No, I would have been straightforward with her and explained the misunderstanding. Leading someone on isn't my style. Besides, I knew you were my match that day you mentioned spice. When did you know?"

I'm happy that he wouldn't have led anyone on. That is the Seb I've come to know. "I think I always knew, but I didn't want to ask because of the rules. And by pretending I didn't know, it allowed me to have this relationship with you that was forbidden. But now it's not. However, with the Soy Joy campaign going full bore, we don't have much time to see each other anyway, so this is perfect," I reply, leaning closer to him, drawn by an invisible force that seems to connect us.

"It is," he says.

I glance around, taking in the romantic atmosphere he's created just for me. "Candles? Haven't you learned your lesson?"

He winks. There's a dare in his smile. "Thought we'd raise the stakes. If the house is still here by dessert, we'll call it a win."

I nod, trying to look stern. "Well, the dinner better be

spectacular." Right on cue, my stomach growls, a traitorous rumble demanding culinary excellence. "If we survive and the food's bad, I'm rating this date one star on Yelp."

Seb's laugh is a song that warms the spaces of my heart I didn't know were cold. He offers his hand. "Duly noted. Shall we move to the dining room?"

I nod with a broad and genuine grin and take his hand, feeling a jolt of electricity at the contact. He guides me to the table, and what I see there takes my breath away. An extravagant spread of Thai dishes, each more colorful and aromatic than the last, is laid out before us. It's a feast fit for royalty, a lavish display of gastronomic delights.

"I love the fragrance of Thai cooking. You almost don't need to eat it to subdue your hunger. How did you know all my favorites?" I ask, my voice a mix of surprise and delight.

Seb winks. "I didn't, but I figured if I ordered every vegan dish available, I'd have a good chance of hitting the mark."

As we settle into our seats, surrounded by the tantalizing aroma of spices and herbs, it's not just the food that touches my heart but the thoughtfulness behind it. Seb made this evening special, and for a moment, all the secrecy and tension of our blossoming workplace romance is worth it.

I mentally commit myself not to burn down his house because, if this is the start of our dating adventures, I can hardly wait for what's next.

Our meal is a symphony of flavors and laughter, the conversation flowing as effortlessly as the wine. We deliberately avoid any mention of work, choosing instead to explore each other's pasts—travel experiences that shaped us, childhood memories that still bring a smile, and dreams that twinkle like stars on the horizon of our future.

After dinner, as we clean up together, Seb suggests a movie. I'm curious to see his choice, knowing it might reveal another facet of his personality. "You sacrificed enough eating vegan," I offer, "so pick a thriller if that's more your style."

He shakes his head, his eyes dancing with delight. "This is your night, and I promised you a rom-com." He chooses Working Girl, a classic that resonates with our situation—two people navigating their careers and hearts.

As we watch, we draw parallels between the characters on screen and our lives. We comment and share inside jokes, and the air around us is charged with a growing connection that feels as natural as breathing.

When the movie reaches its climax, Seb and I exchange a look that speaks volumes. The tension between us is palpable, a magnetic force pulsing and intensifying throughout the evening. Our lips meet in a soft, passionate kiss, like thick, sweet icing on the cake of our time together. It's a kiss that speaks of long-suppressed desires and promises of more. I'm bathed in rich anticipation.

We snuggle on the couch, the movie now just background noise, our focus entirely on each other. We kiss, and it deepens, filled with all the yearning we've held back in the confines of the office. It's a moment of pure connection, leaving us both breathless, our hearts racing with the thrill of newfound intimacy—and privacy.

As hands roam and explore, I'm transported back to a stolen moment in my teenage years—Jimmy Stratton's treehouse, the thrill of a forbidden touch, the excitement of youthful desire. But this, with Seb, is so much more profound and real. It's not the hesitant fumbling of teenagers but the passionate embrace of two consenting adults, fully aware and fully present in their desire for each other.

Needing a moment to catch my breath, I excuse myself to use the restroom. Inside, I face the mirror and take a deep breath, confronting the tornado of emotions spinning within me. My mind races with the voices of my ancestors, each offering their unique brand of wisdom.

My mother's mother speaks first, her voice a blend of caution and experience. "Make him do the work of soaking the almonds before you give him the milk for free." Her words, cryptic to some but clear as day to me, are the vegan version of an age-old adage about making him buy the cow instead of giving him the milk for free.

Then comes the voice of my father's mother, her tone soft yet firm. "Every flower has its time to bloom, but make sure the gardener is worthy of caring for the root." I've always interpreted her words to prioritize my pleasure, but now I wonder if there's more to it.

When I return to the living room, I find Seb asleep on

the couch. His peaceful face, illuminated by the soft light of the TV screen, sparks a squeeze in my chest.

I debate whether to call a cab and leave. It's late, and the responsibilities of tomorrow loom over me. But as if sensing my internal struggle, Seb shifts, making room on the couch and opening the blanket in temptation. "Come and snuggle for a minute, and then we'll call you a cab."

Grateful for the reprieve from making rash decisions, I slide under the blanket and let his arms surround me.

<hr>

THE SONIC BOOM of my ringtone shatters the tranquility of the morning. The phone, a sneaky beast, had wedged itself between the cushions. When I pull it out, Mom's face glares back from the screen in high-definition judgment as if she's peering directly into my soul. My heart doesn't skip a beat; it launches into a flamboyant samba, maracas, and all, at the sight of her digital scowl.

Hey, Mom," I say, trying to inject a note of casualness into my voice to mask the chaos of my waking thoughts.

Her warm and familiar voice cuts through the fog of my drowsy mind. "Don't forget about family dinner tonight." My mind races, scrambling to piece together the fragments of reality. I'm not in my bed, not in my house. I'm at Seb's, and it's Wednesday morning—a morning that has already slipped away from the routine we're both used to.

Beside me, Seb stirs, his gaze meeting mine in understanding. I press a finger to my lips, a wordless plea for discretion.

"Listen, Mom," I say, the urgency in my voice barely concealed. "I'm swamped with work this week. I can't make family dinner, but we have that thing on Saturday, right? I'll make it up to you then." I wince inwardly, knowing that skipping weekly dinner is no small matter in my family's book.

"You sound strange. Where are you?" There's a hint of suspicion in her voice, a mother's intuition tuning into the unsaid truths lingering in my tone.

"Where am I?" I glance at Seb, his eyes wide with the shared realization of our situation. It's past nine in the morning—far too late for excuses. "I'm at work but running late for a meeting," I blurt out, ending the call with a mix of guilt and relief. Turning to Seb, I see my panic mirrored in his expression. "Holy hell, we're both late," I say.

Seb springs into action, his usual calm demeanor giving way to a focused urgency. "Okay, you shower first," he says, already gathering his thoughts. "I'll follow, and then we'll figure out how to get you home to change. We can't show up together, so I'll drop you down a ways."

Gratefully acknowledging the universe for Seb's mental gears grinding more smoothly than mine, I blast through a shower faster than a cat fleeing a bath. My thoughts are chaos.

Miraculously, we manage to transform back into something resembling presentable humans. I stride to the hall closet, where Seb stashed my coat the previous night.

When I open the door, a school of trophy fish, in all their glazed-eye glory, come tumbling out in a quiet, scaly cascade. I screech and hop back. Seb rushes to my side.

"Well, shit. I told you guys to stay in there," he teases.

I bend over and pick up a trout mounted to a board. "What did he ever do to you?"

He takes the fish and places it on the shelf in the closet. "He took my bait."

I arch an eyebrow, a smirk playing on my lips. "And here I am, swimming dangerously close to your lure. Should I expect a similar fate?"

His gaze falls upon me. His eyes are like smoldering embers, promising trouble of the most delightful kind. "Baby, when I mount you, it won't be to a piece of oak on the wall."

Heat rushes to my cheeks. Before volunteering to be his next trophy, I yank my jacket from the hanger and run out the door, leaving Seb to laugh in my wake.

We zoom to my place, where Seb executes a parking maneuver that would make a stunt driver proud. I race into my apartment to transform from the morning after to runway ready. Slipping into a black dress and heels, I slap on just enough makeup to not scare small children. Back in the car, I'm the picture of poise—if you squint.

As we approach work, Seb reaches into the back seat and grabs a lunch box that looks straight out of a superhero merch store, complete with a lightning bolt. "I packed you a lunch," he says, flipping it open to reveal little containers of leftover Thai food and an orange. On top, there's a single dollar. "For your juice," he says with a wink. "Be good, and be nice to the other kids," The entire exchange echoes a Working Girl moment.

After swapping numbers, he leans in for a quick but memorable kiss, leaving me with a coy smile and a hint of what's to come.

I step out, watching his car disappear around the corner. Shaking my head at the morning's turn of events, I clutch the superhero lunch box and head toward the office, ready to face the day with amusement and anticipation, so much anticipation.

VICKY'S VOICE cuts sharply through my reverie. Her "You're late" is tinged with both reprimand and curiosity. I pivot towards her, crafting a smile that I hope masks the whirlwind I feel inside. "Ran into a bit of morning traffic," I say, my tone breezy in an attempt to skirt around the edges of her interrogation.

Her gaze lingers, probing, as she launches into her usual spiel, but I'm already retreating inward, back to the memory of Seb's embrace, the laughter that filled the air, and his declaration of more to come. Who knew being contrasted to a stuffed fish could be so sexy? I'm also happy he doesn't plan to make me a trophy.

Aware of the delicate dance we're performing, the balance between our hidden desire and the professional veneer we maintain, I pause to feel his kiss once more before digging into the day.

The present demands attention, pulling me back as

Vicky's monologue blends into the background noise. It's a reminder of the roles we play, the masks we wear, and the reality we navigate. But beneath it all, the ember of mine and Seb's shared secret keeps the mundane at bay, fueling quiet intrigue for what lies ahead.

CHAPTER EIGHTEEN

SEB

As I approach the pit, my footsteps are deliberately muted against the polished floor. The sounds of the busy office space ebb into a low hum, but one voice cuts through distinctly—Vicky's. Her words, laced with that all-too-familiar blend of saccharine sweetness and malice, reach my ears before I fully come into view.

"Liv," she coos, her voice a thick syrup that cannot conceal the sharp edge beneath, "just remember, the day begins at eight and ends only when you're done."

I pause, hidden just around the corner. Although Liv's face is out of sight, I can vividly imagine her reaction—the slight arch of her eyebrow, the faint, defiant twitch of her lips forming into a wry glance.

"Well," Liv says, her voice carrying an assertive tone, "in that case, we might never leave this place. By the way, I don't think even tortured Jackson Pollack created only between the hours of eight and whenever his boss let him go home."

The corners of my mouth lift. Liv's sharp wit reminds me of why I'm drawn to her. Yet, it's disheartening to witness Vicky's relentless targeting.

Stepping out from the shadows, I position myself beside Liv, ready to act as her ally in this delicate battlefield. "Vicky," I begin, my voice even and firm, "Everyone's schedule here, including yours and Liv's for that matter is flexible per company policy. Our team ethos and strength lie in our diversity and varied approaches to work. We are a company of creative people. We have chosen to be creative in how we manage. We need to embrace our creativity." I almost blush remembering embracing and wanting to embrace one particular creative person even more.

Vicky's eyebrows arch, revealing her displeasure at my intervention. Under her breath, she mutters a snide remark about selective policy enforcement, but her voice carries enough for me to catch it. She's not one to back down quickly, and her next move is clear as she leans in closer, an oversized grin playing on her lips.

"Since when did you become Liv's knight in shining armor?" she whispers, her gaze moving between us with insinuations sparkling in her eyes. "Or is there something more to this?"

I meet her challenge directly. "Supporting team members doesn't require a hidden agenda, Vicky. We're all in this together."

Vicky is fishing for gossip, trying to stir the pot, but her efforts are wasted on me. Yet, out of the corner of my eye, I see Liv tense up, a statue of discomfort and unease.

I glance at the lunch box on Liv's desk, now the focus of Vicky's probing gaze. "Is that from our previous campaign?" she asks, her tone dripping with suspicion. "Liv wasn't even part of that team." She turns to Liv. "How do you have that?"

Quickly defusing the tension, I interject, "Liv was just borrowing an extra container in the lunchroom. It's nothing more than that. Let's keep our focus professional, shall we?" I hold Vicky's gaze before turning to leave. "I believe there's work to be done."

As the day progresses, Liv messages me.

Since we can't depend on the app because you're a rule breaker, I thought I'd ask a question. Are you a planner, or do you like surprises?

I consider the question and reply with a message reflecting my appreciation for unexpected delights.

She responds immediately.

While I'd consider myself a planner, I have a newfound penchant for surprises, given how many times I've been surprised the last week. Do you know what would be the best surprise? A stolen kiss in the nap room after lunch.

I hesitate to confirm the clandestine kiss, aware of the rules we set. But Liv lights a fire within me, a desire to break free from those constraints. She's a temptation I find increasingly hard to resist. The rules are becoming harder to rationalize, or maybe it's just the painful memories finally being replaced with something and someone more worthy.

My mind drifts to the previous night as I return to my tasks. Liv stayed over, and we held each other as we slept. There's a tinge of embarrassment at the thought of having fallen asleep so quickly, but also a sense of contentment in the moment's simplicity. Our relationship is unfolding at its own pace, and I'm happy not to rush it.

Lunchtime arrives, and the break room buzzes with the chatter of colleagues. Maintaining the pretense of professionalism, Liv and I sit at separate tables. As I dig into my spicy eggplant and sip my coconut soup, Samantha's voice suddenly directs attention my way.

"Hey, isn't that the same dish Liv's having?" Samantha's innocent yet astute observation sends a ripple of amusement through the room.

I mentally kick myself for this oversight. In my rush this morning, I had packed us identical lunches, a detail I hadn't thought would be so conspicuous.

Liv, quick on her feet, deflects the attention with a casual remark about the popularity of Phuket Thai's menu. We share a brief, knowing glance, and wordlessly agree to navigate this moment of scrutiny with grace.

The lunch hour passes quickly, and I face the decision of whether to follow through on Liv's bold invitation. My better judgment battles against the undeniable attraction I have toward her. She's become my morning caffeine, an essential start to my day, a craving I can't ignore. If she's willing to step on the wild side, I'm going to follow.

Every step toward the nap room is like a step toward the inevitable—toward her. She's the trouble I can't help but chase, the type that promises excitement and passion.

As I close the door behind me, I find Liv waiting, a soft silhouette in the dim light. I join her on one couch, our bodies instinctively gravitating toward each other. Our kiss is a blaze in the quiet room, a fervent expression of our growing connection.

The sudden intrusion of an unwelcome visitor shatters our intimate bubble. Quick-thinking, Liv rolls to the floor and pops up in front of the other couch. "Good luck with that one." I can see her outline by the light in the door. "Whoever it is, sounds like a hibernating bear."

Playing along, I fake a deep snore, a ruse that seems to convince the intruder to leave.

Once we're alone again, I say. "I do not snore."

"Yes, you do." She steps back. "This wasn't wise. I'm so sorry. I am just overflowing with thoughts of last night. We almost got caught."

"We got caught," I say.

"What do you think she saw?" she asks.

"Everything or nothing. It's hard to tell."

CHAPTER NINETEEN

LIV

The memory of our clandestine kiss haunts me as I lay here, the sun's rays creeping through the blinds, casting a lattice of warmth across my face. It's a very different feeling from the cold confusion knotting my insides. How did I let myself get here, shrouded in bed sheets instead of professional attire, calling in sick when it's my self-control that is ill? I broke my own rule and fear that I'll do it again.

On the way home last night, I called Junie, and we discussed it. She likened me and Seb to flies and sticky paper and said if we stayed in the same room, we'd eventually find ourselves stuck, so I'm pulling away to gain clarity. Fish eat flies and then end up on a plaque on a wall.

Seb's name flashes on my phone and my heart stutters. I instinctively clear my throat, preparing a sickly rasp to match my "ailing" status. The performance is Oscar-worthy, a symphony of sniffles and coughs, ready to pour through the receiver. But as I swipe to answer, I realize—it's just a text.

How are you? Need anything?

I chuckle at myself, lying in bed and overacting to an audience of houseplants that seem unimpressed.

I'm okay. I just need to rest.

The truth? Yes, but not complete. Rest from what? From the intense moment that shattered all the guardrails we carefully constructed to separate work and personal life? From the relentless yearning to be near him despite the cautionary voice in my head? I'm realizing what a dangerous drug anticipation can be.

I could bring over some food … something to uplift your mood.

The image of him standing at my doorstep with a remedy for a sickness he doesn't know he caused is both endearing and terrifying. A mix of gratitude and guilt churns within me.

That's kind of you, but I'll manage. Thanks, Seb.

My finger presses send before I can change my mind. It's the right thing to do. We agreed—no office romance, not because we didn't want it, but because the stakes are too high. His policy, our secret understanding, is to keep what's personal away from prying office eyes, especially now that emotions are intensifying.

I toss the phone aside, my gaze fixed on the ceiling as I scold myself. I knew the rules. I even agreed to them. Despite that, I allowed one moment of overwhelming desire to overrule good judgment. Experiencing his lips on mine felt like discovering a part of myself I didn't realize was absent. Let's not forget he went along. He couldn't resist either.

Now, I'm entangled in a web of what-ifs and consequences. I respect his leadership and intent to keep our work environment untainted by rumors or favoritism. And I hate that I'm the reason we're teetering on the edge of a precipice we might not recover from.

I've always prided myself on discipline and on holding the line. But with Seb ... with Seb, I'm all reckless heart and hungry soul, wanting him in ways that go beyond reason, beyond caution. Meanwhile, the Soy Joy campaign pitch deadline is looming, and I need to get on with that instead of seducing my boss's boss in the nap room. I'm suddenly a siren beckoning the ship's captain instead of blazing my own trail.

I curl into myself, pulling the blanket tighter as if it could shield me from my own tumultuous thoughts. I let the silence of my room wash over me, offering a temporary respite from the internal storm.

Tomorrow, I'll return to the charade, don the mask of professionalism, and bury these dangerous feelings beneath a layer of composure. But today, I'll nurse the ache of my impulsiveness and the sweet torment of that kiss. Because even now, amidst the regret and the fear, I yearn for the next moment of abandon and the next.

I drag myself from bed and make a cup of tea. I have a pitch to make. Soy Joy, not boy toy, is calling my name.

I RETURN to work the next day but keep myself busy. The day lumbers on, dragging, while I masquerade as a professional unaffected by the undercurrent of a shared desire. When he asks about dinner, I pretend to have plans. Seb is like a drug I can't get enough of. He's a hit of something delicious that sends me into a frenzy for more. It's better if I don't indulge. Not until after the pitch is done.

At home, I grab my vegan takeout, the container filled with an assortment of grilled veggies and quinoa, as if I'm trying to fill the void with fiber and protein. Plopping on my couch, I survey the kaleidoscopic mix of greens and grains. "Dinner for one, served with a side of solitude," I announce to the empty room. Picking up a slice of bell pepper, I draw a parallel between it and my situation. The outward appearance is vibrant, but inside it's empty, much like the void I experience without Seb. I take a theatrical bite and chew thoughtfully. "Could be worse," I muse aloud, "You could be a dairy-free cheese platter—full of anticipation but ultimately disappointing." The joke is a weak attempt to buoy my spirits, a little humor to lift the heaviness.

The next day, the longing is a palpable ache, a physical yearning that claws at me, demanding acknowledgment. I reach for my phone, itching to break the silence with a call, a text—anything. But I resist because what's at stake isn't just a fling. It's our careers, reputations, and boundaries we're already stretching to their farthest horizons.

When Seb's name lights up my screen with a simple, "How was your day?" it's a balm to the sting of separation. I want to pour out my frustrations, tell him how I miss him, how the week has been a monotonous grey without him, and how even a moment with his collection of stoic, mounted fish seems preferable to this solitude. But my fingers betray my heart, tapping out a detached, "Busy as usual. Working hard on the campaign. Surviving vexatious Vicky." And I imagine him on the other end, understanding what I mean. That I'm miserable without him. I have to give him credit. He's followed my lead and given me space, but is that because he's being respectful or realizing what a liability this relationship could be?

It's a dance of texts over the next couple of days, a ballet of banter that barely skims the surface of the ocean of our feelings. And with each message, I'm reminded of the line we're towing, the precipice we're skirting around.

The week concludes with his voice over the phone, and my heart races. "About Saturday?" he says, and I can hear the hope, the slight hitch in his breath as he waits for my answer.

"I have a family commitment." That's what I tell him. The words taste bitter, like a lie by omission because the event is with family, but it's more than that. It's a gathering where expectations hover like vultures, ready to pick me apart and piece me back together into someone presentable, someone acceptable.

We hang up, and I'm left in the silence of my room,

feeling the emptiness where his voice used to be, knowing that Saturday will be another night where our separate lives continue painfully apart.

The clock's hands crawl toward the end of the week. I'm at my desk when he approaches, his presence commanding even before he speaks. The office buzzes around us, unaware of the currents shifting beneath the surface. "Hey Liv," he greets me, and the familiarity of his voice sends a jolt through my veins.

I swivel around, feigning calm that I hope doesn't betray the tumult inside. "Hi, Seb," I reply, my voice steadier than I expect.

He leans against the edge of my desk, casual, yet every line of his body speaks of hidden tension. "About Saturday," he starts, and I can tell he's trying to keep the conversation light. "Are you sure you can't escape for a couple of hours? I have this thing I'm supposed to go to, but I could skip it and we could—"

The words hang, an invitation I ache to accept. But I can't. Not with the commitment I have, not with the expectations waiting for me. Not with me having already missed family dinner. "I really can't," I cut in, perhaps too quickly, my heart sinking with the finality of it. "Family thing, it's ... it's important. I made the commitment a long while ago. I can't get out of it."

Seb's eyes hold mine. He nods, the corners of his mouth turning down just slightly. "I get it. Family first," he says, but there's a flicker of something else in his eyes—disappointment? Regret?

The conversation shifts to work, deadlines, and

projects, but the unsaid words linger between us, a busy intersection of words, mouths, and bodies just missing each other.

Saturday arrives with the inevitability of a scene I've played out a hundred times before. I stand in front of the mirror, the blue dress hugging my figure. It's beautiful, but it feels like Kevlar, a protection against the matchmaking hits bound to come at me like bullets.

I arrive at the fundraiser, and the air is filled with the clinking of glasses and the murmur of the well-dressed crowd. It's a sea of people, but I'm adrift, alone, despite the bodies brushing past me.

The night unfolds as if on cue, my parents introducing me to a parade of eligible bachelors, each a blur until Blake Waterton. He's the man of the hour in my mother's eyes—the Hendersons' party golden boy. Her matchmaking is as subtle as a siren, her intentions as clear as the crystal glasses raised in toasts around us.

I'm trapped, an experience I despise, as Blake's conversation wraps around me like a well-tailored coat that's too constricting to breathe. His words are perfectly polite, his interest feigned or genuine—I can't tell, and it doesn't matter. Then, it happens. The moment my mother has been building toward—the setup. Blake's arm is about to find a home around my waist, a prelude to a dance I have no intention of completing. And then I see him. Seb. He stands out in a sleek black tuxedo that seems to absorb the light around him. Our eyes meet across the room, and the connection is immediate.

My heart races, and a plan forms. I can't face the

evening alone, can't face the prospect of being paired off with someone my parents deem suitable. Not when Seb is right here, looking at me as if I'm the only one in the room.

I excuse myself and stride toward Seb, my decision made. My arm loops through his. "Play along," I whisper, half-pleading, half-demanding. "If you don't, I'm as good as walking down the aisle with Blake Waterton by the night's end."

Seb's arm tightens around mine, his role accepted. And as we move together through the throng of bodies, my parents' eyes follow us. Seb turns to me, and there's a fire in his eyes, a spark that speaks of something beyond what's happening here. "I don't have to play," he says, his voice a low thrum that vibrates through my core. "You may have avoided me all week, but there's no escaping what we mean to each other. There's also no way Blake gets to have you when every part of me feels that you're mine."

The word "mine" hangs in the air, a declaration, a claim that sends a thrill through me. It's reckless and bold, the opposite of the caution we've exercised until now. But it's what I need to hear, a life raft thrown into the tumultuous sea of my doubts.

We face my parents, his arm around me. We may have to return to our corners come morning, but for now, we stand together, an unbreakable unit in the face of my parents' scrutiny.

As the evening continues, the moment for dinner arrives. The table is set, and each place card is a miniature decree of social strategy. Blake Waterton's name, etched in a calligraphic flourish, sits boldly beside mine. But tonight's script calls for an impromptu cast change. With a magician's sleight of hand and a mischievous glance toward Seb, I swap the cards faster than a pickpocket on a busy street. Seb's card, now beside mine, feels like a victory flag planted on a battlefield of etiquette. Blake has been moved next to Gladys Farnsworth, a nice old lady and crusader for everything from bee preservation to bandanas for balding baboons.

Seb, now unwittingly center stage, joins us with a nod. As he takes his seat, the evening begins. The appetizer arrives, an exotic concoction that's more decoration than food, and with it, my father's casual interrogation. Dad steers the conversation toward careers with the relaxed air of a man discussing sports. "And what do you do, Seb?" he inquires, taking a delicate bite of the art on his plate.

"I own a small business," Seb says proudly.

"Oh?" my mother chimes in. "And what business might that be?"

"Innovative Advertising," Seb states, and with those two words, my world unravels.

My father pauses with a morsel of food halfway to his mouth. "Innovative Advertising? Liv works there, don't you, darling?" His eyes flick to me, then back to Seb, connecting the dots.

"Yes, she's one of our most talented art directors," Seb says, pride evident in his voice, even as he realizes the slip.

The main course is served, a decadent display of culinary excellence, but the flavor of the conversation has shifted.

"So, you're her boss?" my mother asks.

My parents share a look that's part surprise, part concern—a secret dialogue exchanged over the roasted delicacies.

"Liv works for someone else, but, technically, yes." He looks at me, wondering if he's misspoken, but there's no hiding the truth. His signature will be on the bottom of my paycheck. We can package it any way we want, but in the end, Seb is my ultimate boss.

Thankfully, rescue arrives in the form of dessert. It's a fanfare of sweetness, an array of treats too tempting to ignore. Yet, as Seb reaches for his spoon, the air is thick with more than just the scent of sugar. It's laden with the weight of my parents' unvoiced judgment. Could their debutante really be dating the man she works for?

As the dessert plates are removed, my mother's fingers lightly press against my arm, pulling me to the side. "If you'll excuse us for a moment." She practically drags me to a door that leads to an empty ballroom. "Your boss?" she asks, eyes trying to read my face.

I shake my head, quick and firm. "No, Mom, it's not like that," I say, the half-truth sticking in my throat.

"I have eyes, Liv, and that man has a hunger for more than spun sugar on a chocolate mousse cake." She sighs, her gaze still locked on mine. "Liv, it's a dangerous game, getting involved with someone like him. Rumors start so easily and can ruin careers and reputations ... including yours."

I bite my lip, feeling the "but" I can't quite voice. "Seb isn't just my boss."

"Then what is he to you?" she pushes, a note of worry creeping into her voice.

"He might be everything I've ever wanted."

"I thought you wanted to make your mark on the world and create something that wasn't given to you."

I suck in a breath, realizing this whole time that my mother actually had been listening to me. "Mom, I didn't expect this to happen, but—"

My mother shakes her head. "No buts. You don't climb a corporate ladder lying on your back."

Her words are like a slap to my face. "We aren't sleeping together."

"Don't lie to me. I know what I see."

"I'm not sure what you're seeing, but it's not what you think." Anger swells inside of me as I play her response in my head. "Isn't marrying well about the same? Don't tell me you didn't get to where you are by not sleeping with my father."

Her hand connects with my cheek. I stand there shocked before I break away from her, the heels of my shoes clicking sharply against the marble floor as I flee the ballroom. I'm vaguely aware of the turned heads and the hushed whispers, but it's all background noise to my complete heartbreak.

As I burst through the doors into the night, my name slices through the air behind me, Seb's voice laced with concern. "Liv!" he calls out, but I'm running too fast, the tears blurring my vision, the fresh air doing nothing to soothe the burning in my chest.

I hear his footsteps quicken, following me. "Olivia, wait!" he shouts, and I stop, turn, and fall into his arms.

CHAPTER TWENTY

SEB

"Hey, it's going to be okay," I murmur, my voice steady despite the emotions swirling inside me. Turning, she faces me, and, wow, the streetlight turns her tears into glittering trails, like diamonds shattered on the pavement. I don't think twice. I pull her in, placing my arms around her. It's not just a hug. It's my commitment to protect her from anything that could cause harm.

Liv's fingers dig into my jacket, her sobs wetting my neck as she hides her face there. I sense her pain deeply within my bones, pulsating in rhythm with my heartbeat. I don't hush her, don't feed her any empty platitudes or clichés. I just hold her.

We stand there, letting the night embrace us, the city's heartbeat echoing our own. It's raw, this vulnerability, a testament to the trust we've built, layer by fragile layer. Finally, her cries quiet down, and I whisper into her hair, "Let's get out of here, okay? Just us, somewhere private."

She nods, her grip loosening as she steps back to meet my gaze, her eyes shimmering with unshed tears and unsaid words.

I lead her to my car. Every step we take paves the way to recovery and hints at the profound possibilities unfolding between us.

The engine hums to life, a soft sound against the night's stillness. I keep the music off, mindful of Liv's quiet mood.

The dashboard lights cast soft veils over her, painting her features in a dance of shadow and light. She looks peaceful now, yet the ghost of her distress lingers, a flashback to everything she just weathered.

I drive extra carefully tonight, the streets I know like the back of my hand are suddenly feeling new, laden with meaning and direction. The silence in the car isn't awkward. It's deep and thoughtful, like we're both tuned into the things we're not saying.

I sneak a glance at her. There's a softness, a quiet plea for reassurance that she's not alone in her struggles.

We pull up at my house, and I kill the engine. We sit there, frozen momentarily on the edge of something new. I break the silence. "We're here. My place—our haven for tonight." Liv turns to me, her eyes a mix of thankfulness and that spark, that fire uniquely hers. She reaches out, her fingers brushing mine. It's just a touch, but man, it sends a jolt through me.

I lead the way to the front door, unlocking it with a soft click. Stepping inside, it's like we leave the world behind. The warm interior welcomes us, a comfort after the cool night air.

I gesture for her to sit on the sofa, while I go and fetch some wine. There's something intimate about us in my place, doing these everyday things. I pick a red wine—bold, comforting, just like her. Pouring the wine, I hand her a glass, our fingers brushing again, sending that familiar tingle of anticipation between us.

"To us," I say, lifting my glass, my voice a soft rumble in the quiet room. It's a simple toast, but it feels like I'm saying so much more.

Liv echoes me, her voice a whisper, "To us."

We sip the wine, its rich taste mirroring the depth of what's simmering between us. I watch her, noticing the rosy flush on her cheeks, how she's eased into my couch, into this moment with me. It's clear tonight is ours, just us, away from prying eyes or judging parents.

This is a place where we're not defined by who we are outside these walls. Here, it's just Seb and Liv, two people who can't ignore this bond anymore.

She holds her wine, the deep ruby color reflecting the shift in her eyes, a return to the present, away from the madness. I watch her relax into the cushions, a visual sigh as if the couch itself is hugging her.

I sit beside her, close but giving her space, our shoulders almost touching, a buzz of electricity between us. The room's dim, lit by soft lamps, casting a warm light, shielding us from the cold world outside.

She sets down her glass, her fingers lingering on the stem like she's holding onto a lifeline. She turns to me, her eyes saying a million things before her voice joins in. "It's like I've been caught in a hurricane," she starts, her voice a tender confession. "But here, with you, it's like finding shelter in the lashing rain."

"Storms pass," I say, my voice low, filling the room. "They clear the way for something new, something fresh."

I stand up, heading over to light a few candles on the mantle. It feels like a ritual, sanctifying this space, making it ours for the night. The candles flicker to life, dancing a romantic ballet around us. I return to the couch, my eyes drawn to Liv, her face softened in the light.

"I don't want to overstep," I start, choosing my words carefully, "but if you want to talk about what happened, I'm here. No judgments, just me ... just Seb." Liv gives me a half-smile and a nod. It's enough for me to continue. "You're strong, but even steel needs to bend sometimes to avoid breaking."

The candles' warmth fills the room, transforming the silence between us. It's no longer empty but filled with understanding. She leans into me, her head resting naturally against my shoulder. I place my arm around her, making sure she feels safe, understood, and valued.

"That may be the problem," she says. "I'm always bending to accommodate others."

"Then it's time to find your voice."

"I know, but with my mom, it's hard." She tells me about the conversation with her mother, and it breaks my heart. A slap after angry words that weighed heavy with judgment and fear. Did Liv's mom not see her at all? Or was she just projecting the faint whisper of her own lost dreams? We sit there with her releasing and me taking it in.

After, the silence settles around us. Her breaths, deep and even, sync with mine. It's a quiet harmony.

I stand and nod toward the hallway leading to the bathroom. "You could use a warm bath," I suggest. "Might help wash away the evening."

Liv looks up, her eyes catching the candlelight. She nods, her trust in me clear in that simple gesture.

I lead her down the hall, our steps quiet on the hardwood floor. I enter the bathroom and turn on the faucets, watching the water cascade into the tub, steam rising like a soft, comforting mist. Adding a few drops of lavender oil, the room fills with its soothing scent, the air turning into a warm embrace.

I hold out a robe. "For you," I say. "Take all the time you need."

Our fingers brush as Liv takes the bathrobe from me. She gives me a small, genuine smile, and I close the door behind me as I step out, giving her the privacy she needs. Leaning against the wall outside, my mind's a hurricane of its own, thoughts and emotions mixing in the wind and rain of my mind. I hear the bath, a quiet reminder of her presence in my home, in my space. Her being here feels more significant than I ever imagined.

The candles still flicker in the living room, the unfinished wine waiting. But for now, I'm content to be here as a guardian, ensuring her peace.

Later, Liv emerges dressed in my robe. Her damp hair caresses her face, and there's a warm flush on her cheeks. She looks renewed, yet there's a hesitance, a trace of the night's earlier events in her step.

I notice how my robe, at least a size too big, drapes over her.

I rise to meet her, my eyes asking if she's better. She gives a shy nod. She's beginning to find her balance again.

The candles I lit earlier continue to dance and pirouette around the room. It's like the space has become a cocoon, offering comfort, tranquility, and perhaps metamorphosis from our chrysalis of love.

I guide her back to the couch, where the fragrance from our wine beckons. Pouring her another glass, the rich red wine falls like velvet, a toast to her well-being. She takes it, her fingers steady as they encircle the stem.

As we settle back into the cushions, my heart beats with the realization that this isn't just about comforting her in a crisis. It's about crossing new thresholds.

Liv leans in, her shoulder brushing against mine, like an implicit thank you. In the soft light, I see her, the woman who's effortlessly slipped past my defenses.

The silence between us isn't empty but filled with promises and unmet desires.

The distance between us fades until there's no room for doubt. I turn to her, our eyes holding a wordless conversation. It's a dialogue of glances, each glimpse a phrase, every gaze a poem in our love language.

She sets down her glass, and her gaze locks on mine. There's a question in her eyes, a hesitation, like she's on the edge of a cliff, contemplating the leap. My hand finds hers, an encouragement to jump, and I'll catch her.

I lean in, closing the gap between us but giving her the chance to pull away. She doesn't. She meets me halfway, her breath a whisper against my lips. "You said I was yours earlier. Make me yours now." We meet, a gentle collision that says more than her words ever could. She wants this. She wants us. She wants me.

The kiss deepens, an exploration that quickly ignites into something more vital and intense.

I embrace her, drawing her close, and she responds, her arms finding their way around my shoulders. The softness of her skin against mine sends a shiver through me, a tide that's exhilarating and terrifying in its intensity.

As I pull her close, my arms wrap around her slender figure like armor to protect her from anything not part of what is unfolding so powerfully between us now. With ease, I lift her, and she wraps her legs tightly around my waist, her arms still resting on my shoulders, but her hands now clasped behind my neck as if letting me go would mean being lost forever. Our bodies press together, igniting a flame that deepens and spreads with each breath. The heat of our shared excitement sends shivers down my spine as she arches in our quest to fulfill one another. Our bodies, now a forest fire in need of quenching, intertwine, and I feel the blood rush to my core making me hard with a hunger that only Liv can satisfy. I will starve without her. With her in my arms, I hastily blow out the candles and lift us towards the bedroom, lost in a frenzy of passion and desire. Every brush of our lips fuels the all-consuming need within us.

With each step, a primal hunger drives me forward.

In this moment, nothing else exists but the two of us, consumed by raw unfiltered desire. I want to devour Liv, to ravage her until she screams in joy and release, but I can sense she needs something more, a tasting menu, not a plunge into the main course—no matter how hungry we feel. So, instead, I lay her down on the bed with a fierce tenderness, and our eyes lock in a fiery gaze. I breathe out her name like a declaration of devotion, and she responds with a breathless "Seb," her voice filled with passion and surrender.

Desire consumes me, fueling my movements as I explore every inch of her body. With each touch, she responds with a soft moan, spreading the wildfire already within me. My lips leave a trail of soft warming embers down her neck and chest, reveling in the sweet scent of lavender that clings to her skin. My hands continue their journey, tracing every curve and dip, until I can no longer resist. I peel back her robe, first the shoulders, then her full breasts, her waist, hips, finally exposing her jewel-like body completely. She is breathtaking, and a torturer, for I know that I will never be able to get enough of her.

Her skin is molten lava under my fingertips as I caress and kiss every inch of her. I move lower and lower until I reach the apex of her thighs, where I find her open and waiting for me. Without hesitation, I enter her— filling her completely with one smooth motion. We both gasp at the sensation. My movements are slow and delib- erate at first—building up the tension between us until we pant with an ever-intensifying need for the inevitable explosion of joy we both crave as if we will die without it.

She begs me to move faster and go deeper, but I don't want to rush. I need to savor the delicacy that is my body inside of hers, our bodies moving in perfect harmony. I am lost in the sensation, scent, feel, and longing of her. The delicate rhythms of our dance as one propels us deeper and harder into the primal need to quench the inferno we've become.

With each thrust, her body tenses and accepts pleasure, building towards the inevitable moments of release. Soft moans and cries escape her lips, urging me on with the ever more determined movements of her hips. Her words are like a mantra, "Oh God, oh God, oh God," and I feel like a deity as she completely gives herself over to me.

Her breath hitches, and she seduces even the air in our midst by breathing my name in a low, seductive voice. I can't control myself any longer. My hips jerk as I drive myself further into her, the tension building within me, reaching its peak, its hunger sated, my soul filled. She stills, and a deep guttural moan escapes her lips as the core of her tightens and pulses around me. Our delicate rhythms now a symphony of joyful pleasure that washes over us as we finally tame the fire together, for now.

In the moments after, we lay tangled in each other's embrace, our bodies slick with sweat and satisfaction. Our eyes meet, and I see contentment and pure bliss reflected in hers. I hope she sees the same in mine.

This was more than just a physical act. We gave ourselves so fully to each other, baring our bodies and souls.

As I lie next to Liv, I run my fingers along her arm, experiencing endlessly the softness of her skin.

Breaking the stillness, she asks, "Do you think we made the right choice?" Liv's voice is a soft murmur, a mix of wonder and apprehension. I'm struck that while I'm pondering our souls uniting, she's concerned about where this night of ecstasy leaves us.

I turn to her, my gaze steady, filled with empathy and conviction. "I think," I start, carefully choosing my words, "that some things in life are like gravity. Inevitable. With us, "this," we had no choice." I pause, letting that sink in, watching hope flicker in Liv's eyes. "From the moment we met, there was something drawing us to one another. An energy, a connection beyond logic. It was bound to bring us here. We are meant to be together. I sense you feel that too, Liv, or I would have never given myself to you or asked the same of you."

She nestles closer, her head on my chest. "When my mom asked me what you were to me, I told her ... everything."

If a heart could explode, mine just did. "Every look, every touch, every laugh—it's been leading us to this, to the realization of the unspoken and inevitable bond between us."

She relaxes as she listens, her body unwinding with my words. "I love what this is."

"We'll face challenges," I add, "but together, we're stronger."

In the quiet aftermath, I have clarity. Liv's breathing

and the touch of her soft skin speak to a new reality I'm ready to embrace. I am hers and she is mine.

As the night deepens, Liv and I find a cadence in our breathing, a sync that is like a promise. Tomorrow will bring trials, but right now, we're basking in the glow of a new beginning—one built on understanding, respect, and a love that's quietly growing in the moments we steal from the world. For now, let's sleep and dream of what's to come.

CHAPTER TWENTY-ONE

LIV

The relentless vibration of my phone against the hardwood nightstand drags me from the depths of sleep. I blink against the intrusion, my eyes adjusting to the soft light that spills through the blinds, bathing the room in a tranquil amber hue. I silence the call and curl onto my side.

Seb's silhouette is etched against the dawn, his features softened by the morning light. "Sorry," he whispers. "I brought your phone in here because she's already called three times this morning." His eyebrows knit together in a display of empathy.

"I'm so sorry."

"Don't be. I'm an early riser, anyway. Besides, the view from where I sit is lovely." His eyes skate over my bare leg to where the sheets cover my hip.

I take in the fabric's softness against my skin, a luxurious caress compared to the raw emotions that the sight of those missed calls stirs within me.

Before the weight of obligation can settle on my shoulders, Seb's voice cuts through, soft and reassuring. "I had some almond milk delivered. Thought you might need your favorite latte this morning," he says, the corners of his mouth lifting.

"Ooh, room service. Too bad we can't hang a do-not-disturb sign on my phone." I'm touched by his thoughtfulness. The cup he offers is warm, the scent of the latte reaching out like a comforting embrace. "You know, they say the way to a person's heart is through their stomach, but you're skipping steps straight to my caffeine addiction."

"I aim to please."

"Oh, you did."

I inch up to sit beside him and cradle the cup. I look around at his space and see it's a canvas of tranquility. It's odd with the unease that clenches my stomach as I consider facing my mother. Just last night she accused me of sleeping with my boss, and then, I could unequivocally deny it, but this morning is another story.

Do I regret last night? Was it an act of defiance or, like Seb said, an inevitability? I try to regret it for a second, but it doesn't feel right. What happened last night was pure magic, and I wouldn't go back and change a thing. Well, possibly following my mother into the adjoining ballroom, but everything after that I'd do a thousand times over.

As if summoning her, the phone rings again. I glance at my mother's name on the screen. "I better take this, or she'll just keep calling."

"Do you want me to go?" Seb's voice is tentative, laced with the awareness that our intimacy might encroach on personal territory. I shake my head, needing his presence to ground me.

"Please stay," I say, my voice a mix of vulnerability and strength. I shift closer to him, tucking into his side, seeking the reassurance of his presence. His arm encircles me, a gesture that speaks volumes.

With a deep breath, I brace against his strength and press answer, ready to face whatever words spill from my mother's lips.

The phone is cool and slippery against my ear. "Olivia? Where are you?" My mother's voice, tinged with concern and authority, filters through the speaker, an unwelcome echo from a world I'm not prepared to confront.

The question hangs in the air for a moment, testing my newfound resolve. I'm tempted to glance at Seb, to draw strength from his ocean-deep eyes, but I don't. This is my moment to assert myself, my life, my choices.

"I'm around, Mom," I reply, the words flowing more easily than expected. The softness of Seb's embrace encourages a boldness I usually keep sheathed. "Where I am is my business." My voice is softer than my words, a velvet cover over the steel of my independence.

There's a pause on the line, and I can almost hear the cogs in my mother's mind whirring, recalibrating to this new version of her daughter. "I worry, that's all," she finally says, her tone softer, the edges of her command worn down by my assertion.

"I appreciate that, really, I do. But I'm doing okay. Better than okay," I assure her, my gaze locked on the morning light that promises a new chapter. "I'm finding my way, and that's a good thing."

Her acquiescence comes with a sigh, a sound I know all too well. It's the prelude to another plea for compliance. "Your father and I expect you and Seb for family dinner on Wednesday. You'll come, won't you?"

I let out a breath, the kind that's been held too long and that's seen too many surrenders. "We'll talk about it and get back to you." Seb nods against my temple. It's not a yes, but it's not a no—it's a choice. My choice. "We'll see, Mom," I add, a soft but firm finality to my tone. Dinner with the parents. It's like a sequel no one asked for.

"See you at seven."

The conversation ends, and I let myself fall back into the cushioned embrace of Seb's bed. It's a cotton cloud, insulating me from reality. "Well," I say, "if the road to independence is paved with awkward phone calls, I'm building a highway. My parents ... they want us over for dinner on Wednesday." The words feel like tiny traitors unraveling the peace of our morning. "But you don't have to come," I quickly add.

Seb turns to me, his eyes pools of sincerity and something fiercer, something that makes my heart race. "Liv," he says, his voice a tender caress in the quiet Sunday morning air, "since our first kiss, I haven't just been falling for you. I've been landing right where I belong. I'm happy to face your parents." His words surround me. "We should go," he says. "I'm sure they were only trying to protect you."

"From whom? You? Or myself?"

"They love you, and I get that. I lost my father years ago to a heart attack. There's nothing I wouldn't do to have one more dinner with him."

"I suppose, but dinner with my parents is like dining with the queen."

"Will I be required to bow?"

I laugh. "Mom would likely adore that. So, is that a yes?" I tease, a good-natured lilt in my voice, trying to keep the mood light.

"It's a "wherever you go, I'm with you,"" he says, his hand finding mine, fingers intertwining in a vow.

I let out a breath and release all the fears and uncertainties that have been my companions. "Okay then, dinner with the parents it is," I say, a fresh surge of boldness blooming in my chest. "Now that we have that sorted out, what will we do the rest of the day?"

"Encore?" he suggests.

His suggestion of a repeat of last night sparks my desire. "How about we start the day with an appetizer instead?" I tease, and the shared memory of the previous night's intensity is enough to pull us back into each other's arms. The desire is still palpable, but our touches aren't nearly as desperate, and our kisses are unrushed. It's more like building a fire than needing to put an already raging one out. We let our fingers and tongues explore uncharted territory we couldn't reach last night.

Today's lovemaking is a languid, rhythmic dance, a

slow kindling of fire that burns with a steady, deep heat until we blaze for each other. In the aftermath, I say I love you, but only in my head because sometimes too much is simply that, and I'm not willing to ruin everything we've shared, with three words.

Afterward, the shower hisses to life, steam curling into the air like wistful spirits. We step in together, water cascading over us, washing away the remnants of our lovemaking. Seb's hands are tender on my skin, soaping away any doubts I might have harbored. The droplets of water that cling to his lashes are like tiny prisms, the light turning them into a constellation of stars that I have the privilege to behold up close.

His kiss on the top of my head, under the shower's warm rain, feels like a declaration that this—us—is just beginning. In the water, we steal kisses and share laughter, and let the simplicity of the moment bring us closer.

As we dry off, I catch Seb's eye in the mirror. "Ready for the day?" he asks, his voice as warm as the towel he places around me.

"All I have to wear is that." I point to my ball gown hanging from a hook behind the door.

Seb leans against the doorframe, a teasing glint in his eyes. "I was thinking something a little less ... royal for today. I was hoping for the peacefulness of the tea gardens."

I hold up the gown, its sequins catching the morning sun, and I laugh along with him. "So, no grand entrance?"

He chuckles, stepping closer, and plucks the gown from my grip. "You'd outshine the sun, but jeans would be a better choice." His hands are tender as he guides the dress over my head. "Let's get you home and changed." I'm also thinking we need to be fed since we skipped out on dinner and had only wine last night.

TWO HOURS LATER, we are at Golden Gate Park. Only this time, there is no Segway, no pond splashes, or quick escapes that lead to longing. Seb returns the borrowed uniform, and we take a seat with a perfect view of the drum bridge and indulge in green tea and cookies. When his phone chimes with an incoming message, I ask, "Dry cleaning again?" Ravenous, I eat one of Tadashi's famous almond cookies while I wait for his response.

"No, confirmation of our dinner reservation at Rad Radish."

I wasn't sure if I should believe him, but I'd give him the benefit of the doubt. "You know we can go anywhere, and I'd get a salad."

"I'm rather enjoying my new culinary voyage. I'm sure my arteries will thank you." He looks at my phone as it lights up. "Your mother again?"

I nod. "She's relentless. Just reminding me we dress for dinner at our house."

He laughs. "Good to know. I'm not sure I'd be up to seeing your dad naked."

"Me either." We let the laughter carry us through the rest of the day, through strolls under the park's towering trees and quiet moments sitting side by side on a bench, our fingers entwined.

"What did you want to be when you grew up?" he asks.

"Invisible," I say, a smirk tugging at my lips. "That way, I could sneak into NASA, launch a rocket, and be the first unofficial astronaut to doodle on the moon. What about you?" The truth was, if I were invisible, then no one could judge me.

"Batman," Seb says with a straight face. "But then I realized the job was taken, and my only superpower was making cereal disappear."

As the sun descends, painting the sky in strokes of pink and orange, we reluctantly acknowledge the end of the weekend.

Back at my place, the evening unwinds lazily. We're conscious of the ticking clock reminding us that Monday is fast approaching, but we push it to the back of our minds, savoring the now. Seb's laughter lingers in the air, a reminder of our day as we settle into the comfort of my couch.

As night falls, we move to my bed, make love, and steal every second before the dawn of reality claims us.

CHAPTER TWENTY-TWO

SEB

I stride into the building. The place buzzes with the low hum of phones and keyboards, a symphony of the daily grind. I catch Liv's eye from across the room, a shared secret flickering between us before we mask it with the professionalism our roles demand.

Midmorning finds me in my office, peering over the rim of my coffee mug at the cityscape below, the sharp angles and mirrored surfaces reflecting the glare of the sun.

Jen's voice, always a beacon of efficiency, chimes through my speakerphone. "Vicky and Liv are here for the pitch status check."

"Send them in," I say, straightening the piles of paper on my desk, a futile attempt at order in the chaos of my thoughts.

The door opens, and they walk in—Liv with a folder clutched to her chest, Vicky with her tablet like a shield.

They settle on opposite sides of the small conference table.

"Morning, ladies. How are we looking for next week's group pitch?" I lean forward, elbows on the desk, trying to read the undercurrents.

Vicky starts, tapping her tablet to life. "I'll be ready. My pitch is going to bring the house down. It's innovative, it's fresh, and it's what the company needs." Her eyes flick to Liv, a challenge issued. "What about you?"

Liv meets her gaze. "I'll be ready, too. I've done my research, and I think my approach will resonate well with our target demographic without lying to anyone." Her voice doesn't waver. "Being a vegan, I may have an unfair advantage, but it's not a complicated construct."

I nod. "I'm buoyed by the assurance in your voices. Getting this campaign is important for the company." I pause, letting the words sink in. "May the best pitch win."

Their nods are in unison, but the air is charged with a silent standoff. "Well then, I guess it's game on. Right, Liv?" Vicky says.

Liv's response is a soft chuckle, her demeanor unshaken. "Game on," she agrees, her tone light but her eyes telling a different story—one of unwavering surety.

They rise, and as they exit, I watch the differences between them—the way Liv moves with a quiet grace and how Vicky seems to steamroll her way through a room. It's going to be one hell of a pitch meeting.

Later that day, the energy is anything but sleepy inside Liv's compact apartment. We're a tangle of limbs on her loveseat, which seems to shrink each time I visit, the soft glow of the television casting shadows across the room.

"I'm just not sure if she's going to play fair," Liv says, her brow creased with worry. "Vicky? ... well, she's Vicky."

I draw her closer, a pledge to be her safe place. "She might not," I admit, the truth bitter on my tongue. "But you're going to win this with integrity." I've never been so glad to not have to vote. If Liv wins, it's because the team feels her project is worthy, which will mean the world to Liv. It will be the validation she seeks.

Her gaze meets mine. Doubt wars in her eyes. "What if integrity isn't enough? She's not above playing dirty, and I—"

I cut her off with a finger placed to her lips. "Hey, look at me." I wait until her eyes lock onto mine. "You're brilliant, and you've got something no one else does— you."

She chuckles, a soft sound that dances in the space between us. "You make it sound like a superhero power."

"Isn't it, though?" I tease back, offering her a wink. "Liv, you've navigated worse than Vicky's antics. Stay true to yourself. That's how you'll come out on top. But don't be afraid to fight back."

"I'm a lover, not a fighter," she says with a smile. Her shoulders ease as she leans back against me. "I just hate the thought of her scheming," she whispers.

I place my arms around her, creating a shield from the world. "Then don't think about it. Everyone knows who Vicky is. Focus on your pitch and your strengths. You've got this."

Liv's sigh carries away some of her unease. "With you here, I almost believe that."

We lapse into silence. The only sound is the faint buzz of the television. I steal a look at her, the woman who's effortlessly commandeered my heart. We've settled on a thriller, a nod to meeting halfway, but at the first scare, she's suddenly in my lap, claiming sanctuary. With a chuckle, I scoop her up—my own heart racing more from her close proximity than the on-screen drama—and whisk her to the bedroom. "For nerve-calming," I declare, though we both know it's just an excuse to be closer.

IN THE BUSTLING heart of the office the next morning, I find a moment to step aside, phone in hand, to call Ryan. His voice comes through the line, always sounding like he's halfway into a laugh or a great idea.

"Ryan, it's Seb," I say, picturing his grin on the other end.

"Talk to me, man. How are things in the love den?"

I chuckle, leaning against the cool glass of my office window. "All good. Just wanted to see if you've met her yet—Fruit Fly, from Love Bug?"

"Oh, man," he exclaims, and I can hear the joy in his voice. "I'm in deep. We've got a date set up. The app's a stroke of genius. I'm convinced it's run by Cupid himself."

His enthusiasm is infectious. "Are you hooked already? She must be special."

"You have no idea. She's like ... she's like the perfect riff in my favorite song. Just ... fits. Hey, how about you? Things going smoothly with Liv?"

"She's everything," I answer. "But we're still pretending at work."

His tone turns serious. "Careful, man. That's like dancing on a tightrope. Someone is bound to notice something. You're better off coming clean."

I nod to myself. "I'm aware. But there's the whole no-dating policy I instituted and then there's Liv. She wants to make her mark on her own and while she's doing that, no one will believe she's doing well on her own merit if she's sleeping with the big boss. We've done a good job of being discreet." There were a few close calls, but since then, no one has said a word or let on that they know what's happening after hours.

"Remember, Seb, don't let the shadows touch what you've got with Liv. Keep it bright, keep it right."

"Will do, buddy. Thanks."

We end the call, and I tuck the phone away, Ryan's parting words echoing in my thoughts. Even the shadows seem to retreat with Liv, making room for something remarkably bright. It is a dance on a tightrope, but the view from here is breathtaking.

Jen's knock is soft but decisive. She steps in, her face etched with the professional concern she wears so well.

"Everything okay?" she inquires, her eyes searching mine for the turmoil she's so skilled at discerning.

I force a neutral expression, the mask of leadership firmly in place. "All under control, Jen. Just the usual challenges."

She nods but lingers, a sign that there's more. "I've heard a few rumors."

My posture stiffens in an involuntary reaction. "Rumors?"

"About you and a certain team member. Nothing specific, just ... chatter."

Panic and frustration battle within me, and that rope I've been walking on sways. I need to deflect to protect what Liv and I have. "Rumors are just that, Jen. You know how people talk. I'm sure it's nothing."

Her gaze holds mine for a moment longer before she nods and exits, leaving me with a churning mix of guilt and defiance. Deceiving Jen, one of my most trusted colleagues, carries the weight of betrayal, yet I do it for a greater purpose.

As I sit alone, the weight of my deception weighing on my shoulders, a startling realization dawns. I didn't just lie to protect something. I lied to protect someone I love. Love and Liv intertwine in my thoughts, and it's in this quiet moment of reflection I acknowledge the truth I've been dancing around.

I love her.

The confession, even in the silence of my mind, is both terrifying and exhilarating.

The day slogs on, with subtle glances of longing across the lunchroom and "miss you" texts sent regularly. Normally, we'd rush to the designated house for dinner and pleasure, but tonight is supper with her parents, so I pick her up down the block and head to her place to change.

The atmosphere is thick with anticipation as Liv and I scramble into her apartment, the promise of an over-the-top dinner with her parents spurring us into a frenzy of preparation. We're not just dressing up. We're making a bold statement against the scrutiny and expectations that plague Liv.

I watch, a blend of amusement and awe, as she pulls out the most extravagant silver gown from her closet—a masterpiece of fabric that cascades to the floor, shimmering with every movement of the hanger. "This should make an impression," she says with a glint in her eye.

Her dress is a vision, and as she steps into it, the transformation is breathtaking. "You look like royalty," I say, the words an understatement.

She laughs, a sound that fills the room with light. "If they want a show, I'll give them one." She puts on full-length gloves and reaches for the final touch—a tiara, delicate and dignified—setting it upon her head like a crown. "How's that for dressing for dinner?"

Her spirit is infectious. "Absolutely stunning. They won't know what hit them."

My turn is less dramatic, but no less important. I slip into a tailored coat and tails, the fabric stiff and formal. It's not my usual style, but tonight, it's armor. It's a way to stand beside Liv as her equal.

As we go to her parents' house, the city's twilight

surrounds us, the streets blurring as we drive. Liv's hand finds mine, an unspoken pact forming in that small touch.

As we pull up to her childhood home, we step out, united, a couple not just dressed for dinner but dressed for defiance.

The door to Liv's parents' house swings open, revealing the opulent foyer bathed in the warm light of the chandelier overhead. Her parents stand there, a picture of upper-class decorum, but as their eyes take in our attire, their expressions shift from expectation to outright astonishment.

"Olivia, Seb," her mother begins, her voice trailing off as she struggles to mask her surprise. "You're certainly ... dressed."

Liv's chin lifts in a subtle but defiant gesture. "We were told to dress for dinner. Lord knows I don't want to continue to be a disappointment."

There's tension, a tangible entity in the air, but Liv strides forward, the train of her gown whispering across the marble floor. I follow, the tails of my coat brushing behind me, every step affirming our solidarity. I can't see how Liv could be a disappointment in any scenario. Dressed in flannel pajamas and bunny slippers, she'd still own the room with her smile alone.

Dinner is served in the grand dining room, a space that feels more like a museum than a place for a family meal. We're seated at a long table, Liv's dad at the head, her mother to his right, and Liv and I sit side by side on her father's left.

The evening begins with an appetizer of stuffed

mushrooms and talk of the weather, then leads into a ratatouille and a full-on interrogation. "Sebastian, your company," he starts, his tone deceptively casual. "We've heard some concerning rumors."

The conversation veers dangerously, with pointed questions about my business and veiled implications about my suitability. Liv's hand finds my knee under the table, a message of support.

I'm on the edge of my seat when her mom drops the bombshell. "We had a background check done, and all is not as it seems in Mr. Blackthorne's world," she says, eyes glinting like she's just won bingo night. Panic scuttles down my back. A background check? What could they have found? My most criminal activity is jaywalking and occasionally forgetting to floss. There was that overdue library book from '09, but I paid the fine. The words "background check" bounce around my skull like a pinball machine stuck on tilt. Who on earth orders a background check, let alone tells you at dinner that they did?

Liv's expression is a mix of horror and disbelief you'd expect if they'd confessed to being secret lizard people. "You did what?" she gasps, slicing through the silence like a ninja blender through a banana.

Anger flares within me, a hot, protective blaze, but I tamp it down. This is Liv's battle, too. Her parents—stoic, immovable—have crossed a line, and I'm caught in the crossfire.

I want to reach out, hug her, and pull her away from this cold scrutiny. But I can't. Not here. Not yet. So, I sit, fists clenched beneath the table, as a spectator to the scene unraveling before me.

We had a background check done, I repeat in my mind, a bitter taste in my mouth. Trust, it seems, is a currency too expensive for some to deal in. I watch them and see the gauntlet being thrown. This isn't just about a background check. It's a challenge to the foundation of what Liv and I have been building. And they don't even know it yet, but they're not just examining my past—they're pushing us into our future, one where their approval isn't the cornerstone, and their presence is not necessarily assured if they keep this up.

"It's for your own good, Olivia," her father interjects. "His company's value has tumbled."

Liv sits up, the formerly bending steel straightening her spine until she's unyielding. "You have no right!" Her voice, once timid, now resounds with unwavering strength. "To invade Seb's privacy, to judge him based on his financials—it's not only rude but also offensive."

I speak up, my voice calm but firm. "My company's going through a transition, but I assure you, we're on solid ground. No one has to eat at the soup kitchen."

But Liv isn't finished. She turns to her parents, her gaze fierce. "Who I choose to love is my choice. Seb is a good man, and that's all that matters. Not his bank account, not his company. Him. Don't forget that I'm wealthy on my own. Love Bug has done very well for me. It keeps growing, as do my royalties, earned from my hard work and talent. I can choose love over money."

All I hear is that she loves me.

"Your little app thing is good for today, but what about tomorrow?" her mother asks. "We're only thinking of you." Her parents exchange a look. There's an unsaid conversation passing between them.

Liv stands, her tiara catching the light. She's a queen in her own right. "This conversation is over." There's no room for argument in her voice. "We're leaving."

"But we haven't had dessert," her mother points out.

Liv looks at her mother, her eyes reflecting love and purpose. "Mom, I'm not just the dutiful daughter you expect. I have wants and dreams of my own, and I can't live solely for your expectations. You had your lives and your dreams. Now, it's time for me to pursue mine. When you're ready to see me as the woman I've become, not just the future you want me to be, then we can talk."

I rise, offering her my arm, and together we walk out. The drive back is quiet, a shared processing of the evening's events. But as I glance at Liv, her profile illuminated by the passing streetlights, I don't see defeat like the last time we saw her parents, but absolute resolve and tenacity. Tonight, she fought for herself, and she battled for us, and that's worth more than any approval her parents could offer.

We arrive at Liv's apartment and change our outfits. She's quiet, her movements slow and deliberate, as if trying to piece together her thoughts. I watch her, wanting to offer comfort but knowing she needs this moment to process.

Finally, she speaks, her voice low and steady. "It's like a label they stick on me, Seb. "Permanent child. Pawn waiting for the next move in their game of social standing." And you? You're just the risky stock they're wary of investing in." Her metaphor slices through the stillness, and for a moment, I see the absurdity of old wealth—their love, a currency traded in control.

"I know it was out of line, but Liv, it doesn't change anything about us."

She turns to me, her eyes searching mine. "But it does, doesn't it? It's a reminder that they'll never see me as an adult capable of making my own decisions. They aren't thinking about me. They're only considering their investment in me and how you might put that at risk."

"I think you're wrong about that. I think they'll be thinking nonstop about you."

I take her hands in mine, feeling the tremble of suppressed emotions, and I think about George and his story of how he and Marie left everything to take a chance on love. "We'll make our own way. We don't need anyone's approval to validate what we have."

Her eyes well up, but she nods, a fierce conviction replacing the vulnerability. "You're right. Who I love is my choice. They can't dictate that any more than I can."

I remember that she referred to loving me earlier, but I need the confirmation.

"You love me?"

"I love you with everything I am."

I pull her into my arms. "I love you too."

CHAPTER TWENTY-THREE

LIV

In my studio apartment, the night covers us. The only light is from the city seeping through my single window, painting the room in shades of silver and gray. Seb steps back, releasing me from a hug. "So," he begins, humor lacing his voice, "is it the dazzling view of the alley's trash bins your parents think I'm after?" He gestures toward the window where the faint light plays tricks, turning everyday objects into silhouettes of mystery.

Leaning against the kitchen counter with only the moonlight accentuating my features, I reply with a glint of amusement in my eyes. "Of course," I say. "That, and my expansive collection of Chanel dresses." I motion toward the dark corner where shapes of various garments hang like fashionable ghosts in my closet.

Seb chuckles, the sound soft in the quiet of the night. "Ah, yes, the infamous dress collection. Or perhaps," he continues, his gaze shifting to the open cabinet, "it's your well-stocked pantry I'm after?" His eyes land on the nearly empty shelves, where a lone can of soup sits like a trophy.

I burst into laughter. "Oh, absolutely! My vast culinary treasures!" I play along, waving my hand dramatically. "You've uncovered my secret, Seb. It's the apartment and the gourmet collection of vegetable soup."

Our laughter intertwines, filling the apartment with happiness that pushes back the night. We find a moment of joy in the small, cluttered space. This connection thrives in shared humor and the intimate setting of my little world.

In the hush that follows our laughter, my gaze drops to my hands, a seriousness creeping into my posture. The city lights cast long monochrome shapes across the room, setting the stage for the confession I've held back.

"Seb," I start, my voice a soft murmur, "there's something I need to tell you. Something about why my parents are ... well, overly cautious."

Seb's expression softens, the humor fading into concern. He leans in, encouraging me to continue with a nod. "Go on. You can tell me anything."

I pause. "There's a reason for my parents' vigilance," I begin, my voice barely above a whisper. "It concerns my trust fund—"

"You have a trust fund?"

"Yes." My eyes meet his. "And it's more than just a small nest egg. Some would call me an heiress." His nod urges me on. "That's the source of their caution. They fear fortune-seekers, which is why I've remained quiet. I never wanted my wealth to be a sword over us."

Seb's fingers intertwine with mine, his touch chasing away the fears. "Liv, I'm here because I find joy in empty cupboards and adventures untold, not the numbers in your bank account. And while I'm not rich, I'm far from destitute."

Happiness fills me. "If we're going to be together, then you need to know what you're up against," I murmur. "My parents aren't like that just tonight. It's how they roll always. My mom wants me to marry well."

The statement hangs in the air, a shared secret now laid bare between us. "And I don't measure up." Seb shifts, his demeanor thoughtful as he processes the information.

"No one but my dad measures up. I think we can agree that would be a bad match," I try to laugh off the unwanted shackles and responsibility of being born into great wealth. "I'm grateful for my life, of course, but I always swore it wouldn't define me the way it does them. And, as I've already pointed out, I'm not dating them. I'm dating you and you measure up more than fine." I lean over and kiss him gently. It isn't a passionate kiss but a heartfelt kiss that I hope conveys everything I feel.

"There's something I've meant to discuss with you as well," Seb speaks, breaking the contemplative silence. "It's about my company." His voice carries a seriousness that matches the gravity of my admission.

My eyes widen. The lively banter of earlier is now replaced by a genuine cloud of worry. "What's going on, Seb? Is everything okay?"

He sighs, running a hand through his hair. "Your

parents weren't far off. Innovative Advertising is in trouble," he confesses, his gaze meeting mine. "Everything's riding on the Soy Joy campaign. If we don't land this account, I might have to downsize or close down the road. The current client roster won't sustain the business that was built before my business partner took off."

Seb's words crash over me like an icy wave, and the reality of his situation sinks in. "Oh, Seb," I murmur, moving closer until our bodies touch. "I didn't know it was that serious."

He offers a somber expression. "Yeah, well, I didn't want to worry you. But it's pretty bad. I've put everything into this. My heart, my soul, even my sanity some days. When Brad left, he took half of everything from capital to contracts, to employees, and it's been tough running an entire company on half the resources. Some contracts and employees were worth more than others. He was disingenuous and I didn't lawyer up enough. I put too much faith in an old friend. He ended up with more than his fair share. I could fight it in court or focus on the business. I couldn't do both."

I reach out, my hand gently squeezing his. "We'll land this account. I guarantee you that."

"Thanks. That means a lot. That's why I hired you. Not for the trust fund I didn't know you had, but because you're brilliant, and your talent is something I need right now."

"Whatever happens, we'll face it as a team. Your dream is my dream now."

Our eyes lock, a pact forming. And as the night deepens, our resolve solidifies. We will navigate it side by side, no matter the outcome.

"You know," he says, his voice steady, "this talk of trust funds and failing businesses—it's significant stuff. But it's made me realize something important." He pauses, his eyes searching mine for understanding.

"What's that?" I lean in, my curiosity piqued.

"That we need to be open with each other, completely," Seb continues, his gaze unwavering. "If we're going to be partners, both in business and life, we need to trust each other. With everything."

I nod, my heart fluttering with a cocktail of emotions. "I agree. No more secrets, no holding back. If we're in this together, it's all or nothing."

"Exactly. And speaking of openness, there's something else I should mention." He takes a deep breath, bracing himself for what he needs to say. "There are rumors, Liv. About us. They've been flying around."

A twinge of unease grips me. "Rumors? What kind?"

He shrugs. "The typical office chitchat that we're more than coworkers. That kind of thing. The problem is, it's true. Jen told me, and I told her it was just gossip, which made me feel guilty for lying to her."

"Well, they're right. We are more than just colleagues."

"True. But it's not something we've made public, and I'm not sure we should just yet. Not until after the pitch. The last thing we need is people thinking you won because of your relationship with me."

"I agree." I consider his words, my mind racing with

the implications. "I want to … no, have to win on my own merit."

He reaches for my hand. "Let's make a plan. Once the pitch is finished, we'll set the record straight. Together."

In the stillness of the night, Seb and I stand closer, our hands joined—a symbol of the pact we've just formed. The room seems smaller as if our confessions have pulled the walls in, crafting an intimate world just for us.

"So, we have a plan." Breaking the silence, my voice carries a blend of determination and a twinge of nerves. "After the pitch, we go public and face whatever comes our way. But until then—"

"Until then, we keep it quiet," Seb finishes, his thumb caressing my hand in comforting strokes. "It's not ideal, I know. Keeping this secret is like we're denying a part of ourselves, a piece of what we could be."

I let out a big sigh, wishing we didn't have to keep up the pretense. "It's like we're playing hide and seek, and I'm no good at hiding, Seb." I catch his eye, a chuckle shaking my frame. "You know, I always got found first in hide and seek when I played with the household staff as a kid. Every single time."

"Oh? And why is that?" Seb's eyebrow quirks up, his interest piqued.

I nuzzle closer, the secret spilling out in a soft confession. "I always hid in the same spot—the pantry. But can you blame me? That's where the cookies were." I shrug, a playful smile dancing on my lips. "If you're going to hide, might as well be in a place with snacks, right?"

Seb laughs, the sound deep and resonant, and it's like a warm blanket over the both of us. "You and your cookies," he says, pulling me in for a bear hug.

"But now I don't want to hide. I want to shout it from the rooftops."

"Me too, and we will," he says, his voice steady. "For now, we'll move forward independently but know inside we are the dynamic duo against the world."

I laugh, filled with affection. "Dynamic duo, huh? I like the sound of that. Don't forget, every Batman needs his Robin." I nudge him playfully, the tension of earlier easing into comfortable camaraderie.

We stand there for a moment longer. As we finally turn away from the window, ready to face the hours of sleep before the dawn of a new day, there's a palpable sense of anticipation between us. The pitch, the public reveal, the future—it all lies ahead.

We prepare for bed in a comfortable silence, the ease between us a testament to the trust and understanding we've cultivated. As we lie down together, a sense of peace settles over us.

Our conversation turns softer, more intimate, as we share whispers of dreams and fears, the future, and the past. It's as if the night has opened a doorway to our souls, allowing us to see each other in a raw, unfiltered light.

Our hands remain entwined as sleep finds us. It's a physical connection that mirrors our forged emotional bond.

Morning light eventually creeps through the curtains. As we stir awake, our eyes meet, conveying a message

without words, a knowing that speaks of comfort, understanding, and a shared journey just beginning.

We rise, facing the day not as two individuals but as a
united front, ready to tackle whatever challenges lie
ahead. The previous night's confessions and vows echo in
our minds, a steady rhythm guiding our steps.

As Seb and I leave the apartment together, stepping
out into the city, we do so with a renewed sense of
purpose. The world was the same as it had been the day
before, but for us, everything has changed. We are partners in every sense, our lives intertwined by chance and
choice, and we are ready to face the future, come
what may.

CHAPTER TWENTY-FOUR

SEB

I push the conference room door open, stepping from the cool hallway into the noticeably warmer and buzzing atmosphere inside.

It's showtime at Innovative Advertising. I haven't seen Liv in days. She has been isolating herself, working diligently on her campaign, staying up late, and probably surviving solely on her unwavering determination and quinoa. Her dedication is something else. It's like she is trying to channel the product's soul into her pitches, and this one's close to her heart.

As I settle into a chair, I think about how important this is to her. Veganism isn't just a diet for Liv. It's her creed. I'm genuinely curious about the spin she will put on Soy Joy. On the other hand, Vicky is all about the win, not the why. She bulldozes through projects with sheer force, not finesse. Both processes can be effective when applied correctly.

They are like night and day—Vicky is like a swarm of

hornets, while Liv is a calm, purposeful, and serene field of sunflowers, nourishing and strong.

Vicky swaggers into the conference room like she's on a runway, not a single hair out of place, her heels clicking a commanding rhythm against the floor. She's dressed to kill, a power suit hugging her frame as if her outfit alone could sway the votes. The team's already here, an array of expectant faces around the long table, their eyes tracking Vicky's every move. There's a certain tension in the air, like a prelude to the tsunami that is Vicky's presence.

I lean back in my chair, my arms crossed over my chest. The rules are clear. I'm here to observe, not cast a vote. It's all about the team's consensus.

Vicky's eyes sweep the room, locking onto each team member with a stare that's part command, part threat. It's like she's demanding, "Vote for me or else." Her gaze is a weapon, and she wields it expertly.

"Ladies and gents," she announces, and her voice isn't just heard, it ricochets off the walls like a sonic boom in a silent auction.

"Scrap whatever cookie-cutter ideas you've been fed about treats. Our Soy Joy Snacks? They're not just the icing on the cake. They're the whole darn bakery." Her expression is all shark, all challenge, as she points to the artwork—a neon green soybean with biceps that Arnold would envy and shades that belong in a '90s music video.

"Picture this," she says, painting every word in technicolor, "a bite of the future. Each cookie doesn't just crumble. It launches you straight to the "cool" table. Our tagline? "Get Soy-tastic, Get Fantastic." It's not just a catchphrase—it's a battle cry for the hip, the now, the trendsetters."

She leans in, a conspiratorial whisper that somehow every ear catches. "Let the non-vegans turn green—well, greener—with envy. Because who needs authenticity when you've got this much swagger?"

She punctuates her pitch with a broad, victorious grin as if she's already won. And as if on cue, the room erupts into applause. The sound is loud, almost too enthusiastic, and I sit there, dumbfounded. The pitch was a disaster, wasn't it? The concept, the artwork—it's all wrong. She didn't even bother showing how the concept would be applied across different media—not a single storyboard—just a crazy neon well-muscled bean? Yet here they are, clapping like she's just delivered her acceptance speech and thanked each of them at the annual Clio Awards for advertising excellence.

I rub at the bridge of my nose, squinting against the bright lights. Am I going mad? I've been in this game long enough to know a bad pitch when I see one. But then again, when Vicky's involved, the game rules bend. At least she didn't serve the cookies with a side of milk—that would've been the cherry on top of this surreal sundae.

Liv takes the stage, like the first warm sunlight spilling into a dim room. There's an innate grace about her, a quiet strength that commands attention without demanding it. She's been nurturing this Soy Joy campaign like a gardener tends to a rare flower, and it's clear in every measured step, every thoughtful word.

Liv stands ready, the colors behind her popping—a

simple scene with a Soy Joy cookie front and center. "Think of a cookie," she says, clear and smooth, "that fills you up in more ways than one."

She opens her hands as if she's offering a gift. "Our Soy Joy cookies are different. They're made with care, with the best of what the Earth gives us. They're about eating well and doing good—loving our bodies and planet. Picking Soy Joy means choosing more than a snack." She gestures toward the cookies. "They're good for you, good for the Earth. That's our promise. "Soy Joy —where every cookie is a delicious step to a better future."" The pitch is straightforward and as easy to digest as the cookies themselves.

The room falls silent, not the respectful hush of admiration but the quiet of pre-decided verdicts. I see the light flicker in Liv's eyes, an acknowledgment of her uphill battle. She's put her heart on the line, only to have it weighed against Vicky's intimidation tactics.

Then, cutting through the stillness, Vicky's voice slithers out, cruel and mocking. "Well, it's clear who won. It's a good thing the boss doesn't get to vote. We all know who'd win if he did. Some of us work our way to the top, and some of us do the backstroke if you know what I mean."

My stomach churns at the barb, a twisted knife in a painful moment. "That's enough," I demand.

Liv's poise doesn't waver, her voice steady and true. She looks to me as if to ask for permission to be honest and then shakes her head, knowing she doesn't need it. "It's true, we are in a relationship, but that has no bearing on our work, or the decisions made here. Seb didn't cast a vote because his integrity wouldn't allow it—his respect for me, the business, and every person in this room runs too deep to let personal feelings cloud his judgment." She stands defiant, her conviction a beacon against the shadow of doubt. "If you believe that pitch is a winner... for Soy Joy and all of us" Liv looks at Vicky. "Then I lost fair and square." She waits for a moment to see if anyone denies Vicky's win, but no one does. She gathers her materials and exits the room. I follow, a sense of unease growing with each step. Her composure seems to falter just slightly, a small crack in her spirit. She makes her way to her desk, her movements slower, less confident.

"Liv, what's going on?" I ask as I approach her desk. She's pulling her personal items from the drawers, her hands methodically placing them into a small box. This isn't the Liv I know, the one who faced her mother head-on. This Liv is in full retreat like she doesn't have anything left in her to fight with.

She stops momentarily, her back still turned to me, then speaks with a quiet finality. "I was hired to do one thing, Seb. To bring creativity and integrity to this company, to elevate our campaigns. And I failed." Her voice is steady, but there's an undercurrent of something else, something like defeat. "I failed you and I failed myself."

"Liv, you didn't fail. That pitch was—" I start, but she cuts me off.

"It doesn't matter. The outcome is the same." She turns to face me, and I can see the resolve in her eyes, a decision made. "I can't stay where I'm not valued, where my work means nothing or can be overridden by someone like Vicky."

"I value you, and your work means everything to me."

"I know you do, but do you think I can stay here after what happened in there?"

"What do you mean, stay here. Of course, you'll stay here. You belong here."

She shakes her head. "After that trouncing in there, it's clear that I don't."

"But your pitch was the best one. I'm giving you the campaign anyway."

"You can't. The rules were clear. Besides, if you gave me the campaign, people would know it's because we're having sex. They wouldn't think I earned it, and that's important to me. I rolled the dice and I lost." The look in her eyes tells me this is no impulsive reaction. She's thought this through, weighed her options, and made her choice. "I'm going to head out, but I'll see you later."

"This is ridiculous. You once told me you could handle Vicky. Now's the time. Fight for what you want. If you won't fight for you, then fight for me. I need you here."

"Can I have a little time? Just give me the rest of the day to lick my wounds."

I can't deny her. "I'm here. Don't forget Batman isn't anything without Robin."

She throws her hands around my neck and hugs me tightly before she gives me a kiss. It's not a passionate kiss, but it's not a goodbye kiss either. It's simply a kiss that says silently everything she said out loud. She's hurt and needs a moment to think. She picks up her box and walks away.

I trudge back to my office, the weight of the day's events settling heavily on my shoulders. As I sink into my chair, I replay everything in my mind—the rules I've set and the careful lines I've drawn to maintain professionalism not to mention avoid pain. The no-dating policy, giving up my vote to avoid any appearance of favoritism toward Liv. It all seemed so clear, so necessary. But now, with Liv's absence, those choices are less like precautions and more like handcuffs.

The door swings open, and Jen walks in, her usual calm demeanor replaced by a blaze of frustration. She flops down into the chair across from me, her eyes filled with concern and disbelief. "You know," she begins, her voice laced with a harsh edge of reality, "when Brad left with Mia, I thought he took all the crazy with him, but now I'm not sure. I didn't say anything after the pitch, because one vote against the rest wouldn't matter, but if you think Vicky's pitch was the winner, he likely took your brain, too. If that's the direction this company is heading, we don't stand a chance. It's juvenile, unsophisticated. Even Vicky knows better. What's she playing at?"

Her words sting, but they also ring with an undeniable truth. I've been so caught up in enforcing the rules, in keeping everything fair, that I've lost sight of what's really at stake here. The quality of our work, our brand's integrity, and our entire team's well-being.

I lean back, my conversation with Liv the other night

about Vicky's underhanded tactics playing over in my mind. Liv's warnings and insights into Vicky's sneaky maneuvers make painful sense now. And Vicky's demeanor during the pitch, that smug assurance, the way she seemed to be silently threatening the team. It was a display of power, a warning shot to anyone who might dare to challenge her. That is not the collaborative working environment I spent years and invested blood and tears to create.

I've been so careful, so determined to do everything by the book, to be the impartial leader this company needs after the breach with Brad and Mia. But in doing so, have I turned a blind eye to the actual problems and threats to our team and work? Liv's departure is a wake-up call, a jarring reminder that sometimes, the rules and policies we put in place to protect us can end up causing the most harm.

Jen's right. If I continue down this path, the company won't stand a chance. It's not just about maintaining order. It's about leading with insight, understanding, and a willingness to adapt when things go wrong or compromise when they go right.

It's time for a change. It's time to reassess not just the rules and policies, but also my approach to leadership. I need to fight for what's mine—this company and, most importantly, Liv.

CHAPTER TWENTY-FIVE

LIV

I shove through the door of Pies Before Guys. It's where the scent of baked goods never fails to feel like a warm hug. Eloise looks up from a mountain of dough with her flour-dusted apron.

"Rough day?" she asks, her eyes soft and knowing.

I slump onto a stool. "The worst. I left my job."

"You did what? What about the man?" Eloise quirks an eyebrow, her hands not missing a beat with the rolling pin.

"There's no leaving him."

Eloise stops rolling and leans in, her gaze earnest.

"Tell me everything," she says.

I eat a cookie while I tell her the entire story, and when I finish, she points to the blob on the table she's been working on.

"Life, my dear, is much like this dough. You knead and work it patiently, and in the end, you create something beautiful, delectable. You don't discard it when one batch goes awry or when you feel weary. If we did that, we'd never savor the sweetness of success."

She gestures toward the tray of freshly baked bread cooling on the counter. "If you threw away the dough each time things got tough, these golden beauties here would never exist. Remember, failure is merely the oven's way of teaching us to persist and never give up."

My lips twitch. "So, I should...?"

"Keep kneading that dough. Don't let some sass mouth tell you where you belong. You need to claim what's yours. You deserve no less!"

Eloise's words envelop me, "Seb said something similar." I pick up a cookie, its imperfect edges reflecting the current state of my life.

Eloise, with a knowing smile, brushes flour from her hands. "Seems like you've got a keeper. What's your plan now?"

I take a thoughtful nibble of the cookie. "I just need some time to think."

Eloise leans in closer, her words imbued with profound wisdom. "Take the time you need, Liv, but always remember, time is our most precious currency. Don't squander it. Reconnect with the dough of your life, shape it with purpose, and let it rise to its potential. Only then will you grasp the full depth of its richness. Life, especially when it comes to love and happiness, is far too fleeting for regrets."

I look up, meeting her gaze, now brimming with

newfound resolve. "You're right, Eloise. It's time to don my cape, go back, and fight for what's mine." I could see Eloise didn't quite get the cape metaphor, but it didn't matter. I knew what I had to do.

CHAPTER TWENTY-SIX

SEB

An hour later, I have Jen send out a message for everyone to gather in the conference room. I lean against the table, trying to appear more composed than I feel.

"Team," I begin, my voice steady, "I want to discuss the pitch war. If you believe Vicky's pitch is our saving grace, we'll proceed. But I need your true opinions. The fate of the company lies in this." I scan the room, meeting eyes that quickly shift away.

The silence stretches until Marcus finally speaks. "What do you mean? Are we in trouble?" he asks, his usual stoic demeanor faltering.

I let out a sigh and nod. "If we don't secure the Soy Joy account, we'll have to consider downsizing or closing sometime in the future. It's about survival now."

Whispers ripple through the room, the weight of our situation settling heavily. It's then I notice Vicky's absence. "Where is Vicky?" I ask, sharper than intended.

Looking more frazzled than usual, Jackie answers, "She's at a nail appointment. Broke one during the pitch."

A nail appointment. I almost laugh at the absurdity. *Really?* I think to myself, picturing her prioritizing her nails over our collective future. No doubt she broke it trying to claw her way to the top. She's only in the job because Brad and Mia left me no choice. I couldn't replace the Creative Director and all the other vacant positions at once. Too much shifted in too short a time. Vicky was able to churn out very decent work with Mia to provide much needed guidance and motivation. Without Mia, Vicky got a little taste of power and let it ride roughshod over everyone's best interests. I should have seen that coming.

"I need the truth," I say. "Did anyone experience any pressure from Vicky to back her idea?"

The room shifts uncomfortably, but everyone remains quiet. "I promise there will be no fallout if you tell the truth." Finally, they confess. Marcus admits to being threatened, Jackie speaks of intimidation, and others share similar stories of Vicky's blatant threats that she'd ensure their time at Innovative Designs was limited or miserable if they didn't vote for her pitch. Worse, she wouldn't give them a recommendation for future work. My stomach churns with each revelation.

Vicky wasn't just stirring the pot. She had turned up the heat too high. It's time to turn it down and get things simmering just right.

"Thank you for your honesty," I say. "This changes

our course. We'll address Vicky's actions, but let's focus on what we do best right now. We need to salvage this pitch, save our team, and prove we are the right choice for Soy Joy."

Seconds later, Vicky rushes in, holding her phone in the air. "A little more notice for a meeting would be nice."

Everyone stares at her, but no one says a word.

Right behind her is Liv, with ten pizza boxes in her arms. She sets them on the table and stares at me. "I've got three pepperonis, two sausages, two everything, and three vegetarians. It's going to be a long night."

"You brought us meat pies?" I ask.

She shrugs. "Sometimes you have to take one for the team, but I fully expect you to donate to Bovine Bliss Pastures and The Porky Playpen Preserve."

God, I love this woman. "I'll write a check tonight."

"Wait, what do you mean we have to work all night?" Vicky asks. "I pitched and won. The campaign is done."

The tension's so thick, you could spread it on toast, and here I am, thinking this boardroom's more Colosseum than a company. Liv is the gladiator I'm putting my money on. She's pumped and ready to go. Her comeback has the electric charge of a storm. She's not just in the room. She's in her element, assurance shining from her like a Bahamian sunrise.

Vicky tries to hang tough, but it's clear her show of courage is hollow, just like the pizza boxes we're all picking clean. Around her, the team grabs the last slices, eyes sparkling, more excited for the face-off that's brewing than the pizza we've devoured. This is more than just a meal. It's dinner and a theater performance.

Liv's got her backbone, an iron rod of resolve that says she's done running. She's a return act, ready to bring down the house.

She looks at me. "I know you're the boss, but can I address this?"

I nod, leaning back. "The floor's all yours." My voice is the gavel, giving her permission she doesn't need.

She doesn't stride. She glides, pointing Vicky to an empty chair. Not the head of the table, where Vicky thinks she belongs, but a side seat demotion covered in politeness. "I believe that's yours."

Vicky's eyes narrow, a predator uncertain if she's now the prey. But she moves reluctantly and takes a seat.

The team's eyes flick from Liv to Vicky and then to me as I lean back, a spectator in my boardroom. The tension's delicious, a secret ingredient not listed on the pizza boxes they're still plundering.

Liv stands there, a picture of poised power as she addresses Vicky. There's a certain grace in her stance, a cool fury in her eyes. "I should've listened when you likened yourself to a scorpion, ready to strike back if cornered. And when you told me I couldn't have what was yours on the first day of the job,"—she turns and points at me with a Cheshire grin—,"did you mean him? Honey, I had him the first night I met him. He just didn't know it then, and to be honest, neither did I."

The room erupts in chuckles, but mine's the loudest.

"Absolute truth," I confirm, nodding my head in amusement.

"We were set up by friends about a thousand times removed. We literally set the place on fire." Liv's smile is a flicker of shared memories, bright and burning like our first date.

"Also true," I chime in. That night was an unexpected spark, igniting something neither of us saw coming.

"Isn't it funny," Liv reflects, her voice softening, a hint of wonder weaving through her words, "that I didn't realize he was the one for me until that very first day at work? But sometimes, fate takes charge when we least expect it."

Her unwavering gaze locks onto Vicky. "And if you believe you can challenge destiny, well, feel free to give it your best shot."

Liv leans in, as if sharing a closely guarded secret. "But here's something to consider. The universe has its own way of restoring equilibrium. You push it, and it pushes back—hard."

Vicky's self-assured demeanor wavers as she sinks a little deeper into her seat.

"So, go ahead," Liv says, stepping back. "Take your best shot. But when you find yourself in a battle against the universe, be prepared for the inevitable backlash. Nice manicure by the way." She turns to me. "Seb, what's next is up to you, but I have to tell you, inevitably it's this self-centered wannabe, or me."

As if there is any question. "Liv, it's you. It's always been you."

"Does that mean I'm fired?" Vicky asks.

I take a deep breath. Who needs television when you have a boardroom like this?

"Fired? You can call it what you'd like." The room goes quiet, tension coiling like a spring. "You might consider it repurposing," I say. "We're starting a new initiative, "Operation Harmony." And you'll be spearheading it. Alone. From home. Indefinitely. Without pay."

There's a beat of silence. Liv cracks a smile, the kind that's both a victory lap and a love letter all at once.

"As for the rest of us," I say, standing up, "we've got a universe to align with, and I couldn't think of a better crew to chart the stars with." I wink at Liv. "Especially my North Star."

Vicky stands, her exit less of a walk and more of a shuffle of shame. I watch as she leaves the building. She knows when she's been beat. And is smart enough to know that trying to outshine a supernova is a fool's errand.

The door closes behind her, and just like that, the room seems lighter, like we've all exhaled a breath. And as we turn back to our pizza and cosmic plans, Marcus clears his throat. "So, does this mean that office romance is back on the menu?"

"I promise not to get in the way of love again," I say.

The room erupts, chairs scraping against the floor as if they're part of a dance. Everyone's pairing off like it's

Noah's Ark—The Office Edition. Marcus scoots closer to Jackie. Jen makes her way to Tom, and their fingers intertwine.

"As for the rest of us," I say, standing up, "We haven't got much time to figure this out!"

And just like that, the room is buzzing with fresh energy.

LIV

I'm standing by the glass wall inside our brainstorming room, affectionately called "the fishbowl," observing ideas being exchanged. The energy here is electric, the kind that could power a small city or at least a very enthusiastic meeting of minds. We're working on a new pitch, and it's like watching fireworks. Everyone's a sparkler, dazzling with their unique light.

"So," I say, "if our pitch was a superhero, what would its powers be?"

"Telepathy!" Mark throws in, "to really connect with our audience."

"And flight," Jess adds, "to soar above the competition."

"Super strength," pipes up Raj, "for those big lifting days."

I sit in my chair, a half-eaten Soy Joy cookie in one hand while the other absentmindedly toys with a pen. My eyes are on Seb, who's animatedly rifling through storyboards like a kid with new comic books. His enthusiasm is contagious, but a familiar pang settles in my chest even as I'm drawn into the conversation.

"I once thought I wanted to be invisible," I muse, more to myself than to the team, "but how would you shine if no one could see you?" It turns out I love teamwork.

The room falls silent for a heartbeat.

I lean back, my forced smile waning as a tide of longing sweeps me up. It's been a while since I've seen my parents. Family dinners, a chaotic concert of voices where I felt like a whisper—never loud enough, and always blending into the background.

The memories are bittersweet. And yet, despite the hustle of life, and the sensation of being a shadow in my home, there's an ache for those familiar voices, the clinking of cutlery, the laughs that filled our dining room. The after-dinner brandy. The talk of mismatched socks.

Boxes from Dior and Chanel are little cardboard hugs from my mother that continue to arrive. It's her way of saying "I love you" without really saying the words.

The irony isn't lost on me. I craved visibility, and now, in these rooms, with these people who look to me for direction, I'm more visible than ever. And still, those designer boxes keep coming, my mother's affection placed in layers of tissue paper and luxury branding, and I cherish them for what they mean, but I miss her.

The ping from our phones is in sync, a digital duet with Seb and I sharing a knowing glance. The message is almost comical.

Your bugs have been set free. Care to see each other again?

It asks, as if we haven't been glued at the hip since day one. Love Bug, the app with more optimism than a puppy with a new toy, has decided it's time to let us out of the doghouse. I let out a giggle.

The challenge is absurd. It's something about a steakhouse, which couldn't be less me, which makes it less us.

Seb's eyes catch mine, and he nods toward the nap room. He goes first, and a few minutes later, I follow.

"We don't have to sneak around," I tease. "I hear the dating policy is banished for good."

He pulls me in for a hug. "Let's skip the challenge and redo our first date. How about we go back to La Lumiére?" he suggests with a hint of mischief in his eyes.

I laugh, thinking we are likely on the upscale restaurant's ban list. "We probably made it to their wall of shame."

"Don't worry about that," Seb says, already pulling out his phone, ready to work magic. "I'll handle it."

"Are you asking me on a date, Mr. Blackthorne?" I arch an eyebrow, the corner of my mouth twitching upwards.

"I am. How about after the pitch? We'll celebrate," Seb declares, with a conviction so persuasive that he could probably sell ice to penguins.

But the "what-ifs" start dancing like a conga line of pessimistic ants in my head. "But what if we don't win the pitch?"

Seb stops mid-swipe on his phone, giving me a look that's part scolding, part twinkling conspiracy. "Liv, win or lose, we're going to La Lumiére. If we win, we celebrate. If we lose, we'll need a stiff drink. Either way, they're serving us."

I laugh. "So, you plan to celebrate our victory or drown our sorrows in a five-star setting? Bold strategy, sir."

"Liv, I'm a man of simple tastes. I only want the best."

"Right, because nothing screams simple like a restaurant with a chandelier bigger than my apartment."

And just like that, the pitch seems less daunting because I've got a date with Seb, win, or lose.

Bring it on, universe.

CHAPTER TWENTY-EIGHT

SEB

I'm shifting gears down the familiar streets, the cityscape blurring into a backdrop for my thoughts. I've got something up my sleeve today, a surprise for Liv that I hope will mean more to her than any pitch we could ever nail.

She thinks I'm buried in paperwork at the office, prepping for today's pitch, but here I am, steering toward her parents' place.

Mr. and Mrs. Kato are a tough audience. They did their homework on me and knew about my business before I could say profit and loss. They branded me a risk, not a suitor. But I'm not in it for their approval. It's Liv's heart I'm after.

I pull up, rehearsing my speech. With each step up the pathway, my resolve strengthens. This is not about money or success. It's about Liv and how she laughs when she's truly happy. And while she seems happy, I know she'd be happier if her parents were back in her life.

The door swings open, and there stands Mr. Kato, his eyes a blend of surprise and a measured sort of scrutiny. Clearly, he wasn't expecting me, most likely not now or ever. But here I am, standing on his porch, evidence of the unexpected.

I reach out, my hand steady, waiting. He takes it, his grip firm, an unspoken understanding passing between us. We're from different worlds, he, and I, but at this moment, we're just two men about to speak on common ground.

"Mr. Kato," I begin, my voice even, "may I have a moment of your time?"

He steps aside, his gesture a wordless welcome into the Kato family home.

The grand entrance is lined with expensive art on the walls and family pictures on the entry table. In each one, Liv looks back at me. It's a gallery of her life, and I'm here to earn my place in the gallery of her heart.

We settle at a modest kitchen table. There's no grand dining room for this conversation. It's better this way—honest, unadorned. There are no pretenses, just raw truths.

I start with respect, laying down my cards. "I'm not here on a whim, sir. I'm here because your daughter means the world to me. I'm in love with her." I pause, letting the sincerity of my words hang in the air.

Mr. Kato watches me, his curiosity piqued. He's heard this before—men making promises, speaking of intentions. But I'm not here to promise the moon. I'm here to swear a lifetime of effort, partnership, and love for Liv.

We talk, person to person, about life, love, and the future I'm working to build. Not just for me, but for Liv and any family we might have. It's not about what I've done. It's about what I'm willing to do. And I'm eager to do whatever it takes.

"Mr. Kato, I know I'm not what you expected," I start, my voice steady. "I'm not overflowing with cash, and my business … it's had its ups and downs."

He listens, his gaze assessing.

"But I love your daughter," I continue, "with a ferocity that's surprised even me. She's my partner, my equal. I can't guarantee her riches, but I can promise to cherish her and love her."

There's silence, a moment where I can hear my heartbeat.

"Are you asking me to marry her?"

"No, sir. To ask you first, would be disrespectful to Liv. I'm just asking you to be open to the idea that I love her and that she loves me. I also want to invite you and Mrs. Kato to La Lumiére tonight. We have a big pitch today. Liv would love to have dinner with you, whether the pitch wins or loses. Family dinner is important to her, and what's important to her is important to me," I say, the words holding more weight than any contract I've ever signed.

Mr. Kato's face softens, and I see it then—the shift from doubt to understanding.

"Seb," he says, and using my first name is a victory, "we'll be there."

As I leave, there's a handshake that says more than any background check ever could. Tonight's dinner will be about family, about Liv, about us. And that's worth more than any deal I've ever closed.

I rush down the steps and hop in my car. When I push the accelerator down, the engine's purr competes with the silent scream of urgency inside me. Time is a commodity I can't afford to waste. Every second closer to the pitch winds me tighter.

I skid to a stop outside the Soy Joy office where we're pitching, the car barely at rest before I'm out the door. My thoughts are a whirlwind of strategies and possibilities. I enter the building and there stands Liv, her presence instantly dialing back the chaos in my head.

"You're cutting it close," she teases, her hands skillfully straightening my tie, her touch steadying my racing heart.

I lean into her space, her lips meeting mine in a kiss that's a potent mix of luck and love.

That's when he steps into view—Brad, the ghost of competition past, with Mia, his arm candy. They embody certainty, all gloat and swagger.

"Seb—thought you'd chicken out," Brad taunts. "If this doesn't work out, we can offer you a job—entry-level, of course."

The old me might have bristled, rising to the bait, but Liv's presence is a balm to the intended sting of his words. Her hand finds mine, her grip firm, her eyes holding mine with unwavering belief.

"He's not worth it," she says, her voice the softest whisper, yet it cuts through the tension. "We've got this."

Emboldened by her confidence, we stride into the meeting room together. The panel from Soy Joy is an imposing jury, their expectations laid out as clearly as the spreadsheets in front of them. They want a winner, and as they outline the prize—the campaign that could be a game-changer—I experience Liv's composure like a second skin. With one final reassuring squeeze from her, I'm ready. It's showtime.

Brad and Mia walk into the pitch room before us, the picture of corporate finesse. They're primed and rehearsed, and as they disappear behind those imposing double doors, a frisson of apprehension zips through me.

Minutes tick by, stretching like hours until the doors finally swing open again. The smug tilt of Brad's head, self-satisfaction on Mia's face, it's all the confirmation I need—their pitch hit the mark.

A twinge of nerves gnaws at my gut as I overhear snippets of praise from the Soy Joy team. "Innovative ... Engaging ... Precisely what we discussed," they say. The weight of the challenge settles on my shoulders.

But then, there's Liv. She's like a lighthouse guiding ships through fog. She squeezes my hand and leads me forward with a smile that could outshine the sun.

"We're taking a different approach," Liv whispers to me, her voice a grounding force.

We stand before the panel, a united front. As we

launch into our pitch, it's like a dance we've been perfecting for years. Liv tosses a concept to me. I volley back with a statistic, and together, we weave a narrative that's as much about storytelling as it is about selling.

Our words ebb and flow like a conversation rather than a presentation. We're not just pitching a product. We're sharing a vision, painting a picture of a world where Soy Joy isn't just a brand but a lifestyle. It's not just cookies but innumerable brand extensions, opportunities for communities of interest to form and join around the unbridled enjoyment of eating and doing something worthwhile at the same time. Communities influence other consumers and so on. Before you know it, you've unleashed organic market growth with the same care and purpose with which you sowed and harvested soybeans and formed them into a product people wanted and needed.

As we conclude, a silence envelops the room—the kind that speaks of minds racing to keep up with what they've just witnessed. We step back, our part done, leaving our words and grand vision to linger in the air like the essence of a fine wine.

The Soy Joy team exchanges looks, their nods cryptic, their pens scribbling final thoughts. "Thank you," they say. "We'll deliberate and notify the winning team."

Liv's hand finds mine again, her grip firm. No matter the outcome, we've done something today that goes beyond the walls of this meeting room. We've proven that we're better together when it comes to pitching, life, and love. And that's a victory.

"See you at La Lumiére," she says. She heads home to rest and change while I return to the office.

I STRIDE into La Lumiére with purpose, the memory of our infamous first date trailing behind me where it belongs. The host looks up, a flicker of recognition sparking in his eyes. His brow furrows in concentration, and then with the ease borne from countless nights of matching faces to names, he ventures, "Mr. Blackthorne, isn't it?"

I pause, considering the weight of my name. But tonight, I'm not just myself. I'm part of something larger, a family gathering of sorts. I offer a polite nod but tell him, "The reservation is under Kato."

His brow furrows in confusion, but I'm not lying. Tonight, more than half of my party carries the Kato name. It's a technical truth, the best kind to evade the notoriety of a past mishap.

With an almost palpable reluctance, he leads me to our table, the same one where Liv and I first sat together. The memories cascade in a rush of laughter, shared glances, and the thrill of a new connection—and yes, the less glamorous fire and flood.

Sitting there, waiting for Liv and her parents to join me, I feel the cycle of fate turning, bringing us back to where it all began, yet moving us forward into uncharted territory. Tonight, it's not about what went wrong. It's about everything that's gone right since.

CHAPTER TWENTY-NINE

I open the door to La Lumiére, the site of the infamous first date with Seb that's made us a legend in our own time. The host lifts his gaze, and there it is—that flicker of recognition, followed by a wary narrowing of the eyes. Great, I'm officially "that girl."

He leads me to the table, the very scene of the ... let's call it "the incident." As he seats me, he plucks the lit candle from the center of the table with an almost apologetic flourish. "Just a precaution, miss," he says, and I swear there's a tremor of fear in his voice. He flees before I can point out that the table is set for four.

Across from me is Seb, looking distractingly handsome in the same suit he wore the first night I saw him. It's one of those moments where the world sharpens, and everything else becomes less vivid because, well, Seb.

He's the type of handsome that makes me do a double-take each time I see him. The handsome that seems to have been crafted for moments like these under the dimmed lights of a restaurant that's probably now updating its safety protocols because of me.

"Hey," I say, my voice steady despite the butterflies doing acrobatics in my stomach.

Seb grins, and I'm reminded all over again why I fell for him. "You look beautiful."

"Ain't nothing you haven't seen before." I run my hands over the dress, the same Chanel dress I wore on our first date, dry-cleaned and pressed.

"Every day is like seeing you for the first time."

Seb's words warm my heart, reminding me of why I fell for him. It wasn't just the suit or his chiseled jaw. It was everything. He makes me laugh and looks at me like I am the only one in the room—even when that room is rapidly filling with smoke and water.

"Do you think the staff believes we'll set the place on fire again?"

"Well, you look hot enough in that dress that it's a real risk."

Settling into my chair, I glance around, amused to see servers moving with a precision that would rival a SWAT team, snuffing out nearby candles and positioning fire extinguishers within arm's reach. It's like watching a well-choreographed ballet of paranoia.

I lean back, taking it all in—the extinguishers standing guard like sentinels, the waitstaff on high alert.

Our server arrives, his movements stiff, probably imagining his tip disappearing with every candle he snuffs. "Would you like anything to drink while you wait?" he asks, eyeing me as if I might order a Molotov cocktail.

"Just water for now, thanks," I say, deciding to spare him the heart attack.

He scribbles on his notepad and scurries away.

I'm still snickering when my parents suddenly appear, guided by a nervous-looking host.

"Mom, Dad, what are you doing here?"

Dad smiles. "We were invited to dinner."

I look at Seb. "Did you do all this?" I ask.

He nods. "Wednesday's family dinner night," he says as if it's the most natural thing in the world.

As hugs are exchanged, a palpable sense of relief and reconciliation fills the air, washing away all the hurt and anger from before. Mom's eyes are sparkling, and Dad's got that proud look he tries to hide but never can.

We settle into our seats, and the server comes over. We order from the vegan menu, and he glances at Seb, asking, "Hold the tahini, right?"

My mom leans in, admiring the flow of my dress. "You look beautiful, Liv. That dress is stunning on you."

I smile. "Well, I've got a fantastic personal shopper," I say, nodding toward her. "Top-notch taste."

The laughter barely subsides when Seb's phone rings. Once, twice, and then a third time. I nudge him. "Answer it. It could be important." He hesitates, not wanting to interrupt the evening, but I'm insistent. "Answer the damn call, Seb."

He finally relents, excusing himself from the table.

His responses are quick, a "yes," a "no," and a heartfelt "thank you" before his face lights up with joy.

I'm on my feet instantly, a cheer ready on my lips, but in my excitement, I send my water glass toppling over. It's like an alarm goes off, and within seconds, half a dozen servers descend, mops and cloths in hand, their movements quick and a little too practiced.

"We got the contract, right?" I ask, needing to hear the words, to let them sink in, to make them real.

Seb's expression is all the confirmation I need, but he says it anyway, "Yes, we got it! They were wowed by our vision beyond the cookies."

Glasses are raised, toasts are made, and the air is thick with the sweet scent of success and new beginnings. But more importantly, my parents' faces beam with pride and joy. For the first time, I genuinely feel like I am a part of something that I created, nurtured, and brought to fruition—not just as part of a team, but as a leader and a visionary.

Going to Innovative Advertising was a leap, a test to prove myself. And I did.

"So, what's the next step for you two?" Dad asks, his voice tinged with curiosity and the protective undertone that's always been his way.

Seb takes my hand under the table before turning to my parents with a look of resolve. "Well, I hope Liv will move in with me," he says, his voice steady.

My heart races with excitement as I squeeze his hand, unable to contain my joy.

Mom makes a "tsk" sound. "Why buy the cow if you can get the milk for free, right?"

I suck in a breath, wondering if the night will end in another kind of inferno, one flamed by my mother's prudish but protective nature.

Seb's response is immediate, his commitment clear. "I'm all in," he declares. "I plan to buy all the milk and cows Liv will offer. I'll buy the whole damn farm. But you know your daughter and she needs time to make wise choices. I plan to spend that time showing her I'm the only choice."

My mom seems to consider this for a moment and then smiles.

Dad raises his hand, signaling that he has something to say. He fishes out a business card from his jacket and slides it across the table to me. It's embossed, serious, and belongs to the family lawyer.

"We've made arrangements to release your trust fund," he announces, his voice carrying a weight that immediately quiets the table.

I'm taken aback. "What brought about this change of heart?" I inquire, my fingers delicately tracing the edges of the card, hoping for more insight.

Dad shares a meaningful glance with Mom, and it's evident that this decision wasn't made lightly.

"Liv, you've demonstrated your independence and made wise choices in your life, your career," he pauses, acknowledging Seb with a nod, "and in your choice of partner. We should've placed our trust in you from the beginning."

A mixture of pride and a sweet sense of triumph surges within me.

Mom smiles warmly. "We trust you. We raised you to be strong and independent, but we've also learned so much from you. You've taught us the importance of trust, love, and the value of following one's heart."

The revelation of the trust fund brings me joy, but it isn't just about the money. It's affirmation, trust, and freedom. As I look around the table—at Seb, at my parents, at the life we're building—it's clear that my greatest assets aren't tied up in any of that. They're right here, in the laughter, the shared looks, and what lies ahead.

We dive into our dinner, a tapestry of greens and grains that would make any herbivore proud. The servers eye us like we're a couple of notorious outlaws at a high-noon duel.

Mom looks around at the jittery staff and whispers, "They seem ready to jump into the nearest lifeboat. Do you think they know something about this dish we don't?"

Dad chuckles, "Probably on the lookout for that girl who turned the restaurant into a five-alarm fire drill."

I lean back and laugh. I could fess up, but I'll take the truth to my grave. "We should be grateful for their vigilance. You never know what can happen."

As we finish up, the staff exhales a collective sigh of relief. Not a single spark to report.

At the exit, the host gives us a wink and whispers, "Congratulations on a quiet evening. We'll think you're just regular customers if you keep this up."

CHAPTER THIRTY

SEB

Moving day, and here I am, juggling boxes that seem to multiply like rabbits every time I blink. I've got a box in my arms labeled Herbs & Spices A-L, and I'm pretty sure there's another one for M-Z around here somewhere. Who knew that culinary veganism was a branch of library science?

As I trudge up to our shared abode, I swear the boxes are getting heavier. "Hey Liv, are you sure all these cookbooks are necessary?" I call out, setting down a stack with a thud.

From her fortress of ferns and succulents, she looks up, her grin as bright as the sunflowers poking out from one box. "Every single page, Seb. And don't you dare mix my tempeh recipes with the tofu ones."

I shake my head in mock despair. In the last box were enough legumes to start her own farmer's market.

The process is like a well-oiled, albeit slightly comedic, machine. Up and down the stairs we go, her possessions slowly melding with mine. I'm on plant duty now, convinced she has somehow smuggled an entire rainforest into our house. I half expect a toucan to fly out of one pot.

Finally, it's just the mattress left. We maneuver it with the finesse of two people who've clearly never worked in furniture delivery. "Pivot!" Liv shouts, laughing so hard I can barely understand her through the giggles.

"Pivot?" I grunt.

"Just a few more feet." She pushes, and I lose my balance. The mattress flops onto the frame in the guest bedroom, and we both collapse on the soft bed, laughing and catching our breath. Our bodies are intertwined, our energy turning into something more intense. I kiss her neck, and she moans, her fingers tangling in my hair.

"Seb," she whispers, pulling me even closer.

My body is on fire with desire as I give in to the overwhelming need for her. Our kisses turn feverish, our hands grasping at every inch of each other's bodies. The mundane task of moving day is forgotten as we succumb to raw passion. With each touch, my mind is consumed by her, and nothing else exists.

She pulls away, her chest heaving with breathless gasps. Our eyes meet, and I can see the same hunger mirrored in hers. Without a word, we continue to explore each other, our bodies moving in perfect synchronicity.

I am lost in her touch and surprised at how effortlessly she engulfs my senses. In this moment, nothing else matters but the intense connection we share. And as we reach the peak of our passion, I know that this is a love that will always hold me captive.

As we lay tangled in each other's arms, the sun sets and a sense of contentment washes over me. As I drift off to sleep, I am grateful for every moment of pure bliss with the love of my life.

———

THE SOUND of hammering yanks me from a nap that had overtaken me after our lovemaking. Groggy and disoriented, I blink against the darkness, realizing night has already cloaked the room in shadows.

Dragging myself to my feet, I pull on my pants and follow the sporadic thuds to my home office. In the dim light, Liv is delicately balanced on a chair as she hangs my old fishing trophies on the wall.

"What's going on?" I mumble, still half in the land of dreams where the fish talk and the seas sing.

Liv turns, her face lit by a conspiratorial smile. "They're a part of you, which means they're a part of us," she declares, stepping down to assess the newly decorated wall. "But I expect you to donate to Happy Gills Fish Farm."

"Of course." I'm caught between amusement and affection. "Here, I thought you'd suggest a ceremonial release back into the wild," I say, crossing the room to stand beside her. "Or a mass burial in the backyard."

She laughs, the sound warm in the quiet of the room. Then, with a flourish, she produces a tiny scarf and hat, accessories that seem better suited for a miniature snowman than a fish.

She hops back onto the chair and wraps the scarf around the trout's neck with theatrical care, then places the hat just so. It's a sight so ridiculous, I laugh.

She hops down. "Well, if they have to be wall-bound, they might as well do it in style," she says. "Besides, it makes them look less unhappy to be dead." She steps back, hands on her hips, admiring her work.

I wrap an arm around her, pulling her close as we consider the now dapper-looking fish. "He looks ecstatic," I say. "I never knew a largemouth bass could be so fashionable." I lean down to kiss her, thinking how even my fish have never had it so good.

ALSO BY KELLY COLLINS

Love Bug Novels

Swipe Right for Romance

The Dating Dilemma

An Aspen Cove Romance Series

One Hundred Reasons

One Hundred Heartbeats

One Hundred Wishes

One Hundred Promises

One Hundred Excuses

One Hundred Christmas Kisses

GET A FREE BOOK.

Go to www.authorkellycollins.com

ACKNOWLEDGMENTS

ABOUT THE AUTHOR

International bestselling author of more than thirty novels, Kelly Collins writes with the intention of keeping love alive. Always a romantic, she blends real-life events with her vivid imagination to create characters and stories that lovers of contemporary romance, new adult, and romantic suspense will return to again and again.

For More Information
www.authorkellycollins.com
kelly@authorkellycollins.com